The Weed of Earth

The Legend of the Future IV

The Weed of Earth

The Legend of the Future IV

By Luiza Dobrzynska

PAPERBACK ISBN: 979-8-9853307-0-0
EPUB ISBN: 979-8-2013967-0-1
***

WRITTEN BY LUIZA DOBRZYNSKA
PUBLISHED BY ROYAL HAWAIIAN PRESS
COVER ART BY TYRONE ROSHANTHA
TRANSLATED BY RAFAL STACHOWSKY
PUBLISHING ASSISTANCE: DOROTA RESZKE
***

FOR MORE WORKS BY THIS AUTHOR, PLEASE VISIT:
WWW.ROYALHAWAIIANPRESS.COM
***

VERSION NUMBER 1.00

Motto

The stone which the builders rejected has become the cornerstone
(Gospel of Matthew)

A little girl was kneeling in front of the window, looking at the sky in amazement. The setting sun turned it into a daily spectacle, which never happened exactly the same twice. Luminous reflections of different colors lay on her happy face. Pastel colors, intertwining in various configurations, created a multicolored moving kaleidoscope above the line of green hills, which the child eagerly watched through the window, until it was completely dark.

"The sun has gone to bed, it's time for us to do the same. Tomorrow will be a new day," the mother approached the girl and hugged her.

She kissed her warm head, checking to see if the child's temperature had risen. She took her in her arms, laid her on the bed and pulled the soft blanket over her. She laid a bunny made of cloth, filled with scraps of linen, on her pillow

"Mom, does the Earth have a sun too?" the girl asked sleepily, hugging the toy.

"Yes, dear," the young woman replied.

She had dark blond hair, gray eyes and a beautiful, fair face.

She sat down on the bed next to her daughter. She looked at her with boundless love mixed with a hint of strange sadness.

"Does it have sunsets, too?" asked the child, although her eyes were already closing involuntarily.

"It does, of course. They are just slightly different. The Earth's sun paints the sky with bright colors: yellow, red and orange. They are so strong that sometimes it's difficulty to even look at them."

"Are there stars too?"

"Stars can be seen from anywhere, Jamie. From every planet. They are immutable."

"And the moons too?"

"We have only one moon on Earth, which in the night sky looks like a plate, sometimes round, and sometimes crescent-shaped," the girl's mother looked at the view outside the window. "And what we call moons here are actually the two companion planets of our Patris. As you get older, you learn about them at school. They will also tell you about our blue planet, which is mostly covered with water. About gorgeous rainforests that only certified ecologists are allowed in. About how big the cities and countries of Earth are, how tall the houses they built and who lives in them. About highways, videoart parks and manufacturing plants located in the desert. About the dead seas and destroyed continents called Europe and Asia. How people finally learned to live without destroying their shared world and how much it cost. Now, I'll sing you something, so you can sleep easier."

The child was silent for a long time. The seated woman stroked her tousled curls gently, humming a lullaby. She already thought that her daughter was asleep when she suddenly moved and hugged her mother's hand with her warm arm.

"Mom..." she whispered inquiringly. "But you made it all up, didn't you?"

"What are you saying, Jamie?"

"I'm old enough, mom. I'm not a child. You can tell me the truth."

"But, honey...!"

"There is no such thing as Earth. It's just such a fairy tale..."

*****

How lonely does a person have to be to create their own soulmate? Someone to accompany them day and night so that they never feel alone and always have someone to talk to? My imaginary brother was a Mestizo named Silver. Why a Mestizo? At the time, I was fascinated by the Indians. My father, a cultural historian, had many unique publications at home, including a beautiful album of paper imitation showcasing the forgotten Indian tribes. My father never forbade me to browse his collection, so I could browse as many albums as I wanted. I didn't really like reading, but pictures speak louder than words. I would look through them all day, alone in the huge house. Thus, was born Silver, the green-eyed Oglala Sioux, tall and slender as a reed, with black hair falling over his shoulders. One might expect that such an imaginary friend would be the same age as me, but somehow that was not the case. Silver was an adult; he was twenty-one years old. Always... when I was nine, and when I had my sixteenth birthday. That's what I dreamed him like. As to why, it's hard to explain. Maybe I needed not only someone to play with, but also a guardian to protect me?

When, by coincidence, much later I received an android companion as a gift, I began to think about something else. Why is the world in which I was born and raised so filled with loneliness that it needs to be treated with artificial human substitutes? It took me a long time to realize that, unlike my favorite childhood toy, which was the electronic squirrel, the android is not just an interactive machine. Not at all. And that such loneliness may also be familiar to them.

I.

I was maybe eight years old when, again and again, the realization that I was different from my peers came to me. I became confident of the fact that I'm different upon returning from the sanatorium where my mother had sent me. I should wonder why she did that a good year after I left the hospital, where I spent two whole months, and not right away. Because after all, I was very sick, although no one told me what it was. I only remember that I had a terrible headache and couldn't eat or drink for many weeks. I lay under various devices, half asleep and half delirious. When I recovered, I was told that this was a real triumph for medicine.

My mother arranged for the sanatorium for me. I saw this trip as an unexpected vacation and only when I returned, I realized that it was something more. The nurse from the facility, who brought me home, had an envelope with printouts for my parents. Opening it, they both locked themselves in the living room. I was playing in the foyer with my electronic squirrel and was not trying to eavesdrop, but I couldn't help but hear their raised voices.

"It's all your fault!" shouted mom. "You lied to me, and this is the result! I will never forgive you for that, do you hear me?!"

"You won't forgive me for what?! Aurita is a beautiful, healthy girl. Not everyone has to be a scientist," her father replied in anger.

Mom started crying.

"I would never have expected that something like this would happen to me," she lamented. "That my child would be below the norm of our class. Who did I even give birth to? Who will she be when she grows up? I don't want to be ashamed of my child my entire life!"

"But, honey," the father said again. "How is that my fault?"

"You dare to even ask, you monster?! If I knew that you have zeroes in your family, I would never have married you! And on top of that, I find out that one of your sisters sat in a mental asylum! You hid that from me."

"Give me a break, Carmen Antonio, what does the zero of genetic usefulness in one of my sisters and a nervous breakdown in the other have to do with Aurita's test results? What does the infectious disease, which our daughter suffered, have to do with the grade zero classification of my sister? Besides, these are two different matters, fertility and IQ..."

"If it wasn't connected, the zeroes wouldn't be so despicable in public view! And even at Aura Maria's birth, the doctors warned me about her hardships! Don't put all the blame on the disease! You know full well that we should have given her away immediately!"

"Shut up, woman!"

I didn't understand much of this exchange. I was too young to understand the stigma of having a member of the family with the classification of zero fertility, or worse, being someone like that. Regardless, I deduced from my mother's tone that she harbored a grudge against me and I was about to cry. At such a young age, that is the only protection one can have. When Mom opened the living room door, I was ready for the tears, but they got stuck in my throat as soon as I looked at her face. She looked at me with anger and disgust, as if I was a rotting carcass. She walked past me without a word and locked herself in her room.

Only after a while did father leave the living room. He was walking towards his office, but when he saw me, he stopped.

"Were you eavesdropping, Aura Maria?

I shook my head in silence. He sighed and crouched down next to me. I snuggled into his arms, into a shirt that smelled of pipe smoke. He stroked my head gently.

"Dad, why doesn't mom love me?" I asked quietly. He shuddered.

"Don't say that, honey. It's not true. Mom is just angry, that's why she said all these things that she doesn't mean at all. Tomorrow it will all pass."

He probably didn't believe that himself. He hugged me and held me as if afraid that I might suddenly slip away from him.

"Tomorrow everything will calm down."

He lifted me up and carried me to bed.

"Sleep now, princess. It's late. Tomorrow will be a new day and everything will go back to the way it was."

He really wanted to believe it, and so did I. I obediently covered myself with the blanket and closed my eyes. Father kissed my forehead, turned off the light and left. I was left alone with my thoughts, and I didn't feel like sleeping at all. After a while, my squirrel ran up and jumped on my pillow, curling up into a ball next to my ear. Although I was still a child and knew little about the world, I knew that my pet was an artificial creation. However, I loved Rudzia like a living person. That night, I realized why I was so attached to her. She was the only one who played with me – I didn't have any friends, even though I went to a school with so many children. They didn't want to play with me, and I had the feeling that I wasn't allowed to talk to them. Their parents looked at me with superiority, unpleasantly.

For the first time, I thought that maybe it has something to do with my academic performance, which was in fact very poor. Could my illness have influenced that? At the beginning of the year, the teachers treated me like all the other students, then they stopped picking me for answers, they no longer encouraged me to read my homework out loud or gave me school assignments. I was glad about it – being called to the blackboard was a nightmare for me, I immediately turned into the proverbial pillar of salt, and it was impossible to draw out a single meaningful word from me. I felt the happiest when no one paid attention to me. That night I realized it was not normal.

In the morning, contrary to my father's words, nothing was fine. It turned out that at night my mother packed her suitcase and left, leaving only a short note on the table, stating that *she must think it over*. I didn't know what exactly. My father was clearly upset and tried to hide it from me as best he could. Of course, I knew certain things, even though I was silent and pretended that everything was fine. I tried to cheer him up with childish pranks, for which I had enough time – he never sent me to school again. I thought that he wanted me to be with him because he felt sad after the quarrel with mother, no other reason came to my mind, and I liked this unexpected extension of my vacation. When you're eight years old, everything seems simple and natural.

Mom returned a week later. It was six in the morning and I was still in bed when I heard her voice in the hallway. I jumped up and walked barefoot to the door. I've never done this before, but previous experience has taught me that eavesdropping could be very helpful. Holding my breath, I put my ear to the door.

"I hope you've cleared your head," father said. There was relief in his voice, mixed with feigned strictness.

"It's not like that, Johnny," mother took a deep breath. "I want to give us another chance."

"What?!"

"Don't raise your voice at me. You know very well that we haven't gotten along for a long time. And you also know why."

"You're not serious."

"I am completely serious. Look at these papers, this is the best solution to our problems. The educational center. They will take care of her there, teach her a profession, and we will be able to try again."

Father was breathing heavily, so loudly that I heard it from where I stood. When he finally spoke, his voice trembled with anger.

"I will never allow that. What kind of mother are you, Carmen Antonio?

"Mother, mother... that's what I'm saying! I don't want to be associated with such a creature. Do you understand that, having received these results, no genetic committee would recognize her as a full citizen? Hah, not even a human being. Do you understand? I am the mother of... a plant!"

I bit my fingers subconsciously. I understood little from this exchange, but I realized that it was in some way unbeneficial for me. From the corridor I heard the sounds of a struggle and again the voice of my father:

"Get out of here! I don't want to see you again near this house. You are not going to waste away my daughter, do you hear me?!"

I jumped away from the door and rushed to the bed, while Rudzia, curled up on my pillow as usual, jumped up, puffing out her tail. I threw a blanket over my head and began to cry. The squirrel circled chaotically around me, its tiny brain with a dozen processors struggling to decide what to do. I cried until my father showed up in my room. He took me in his arms and rocked me back and forth for a long while.

"Don't cry," he said. "I won't let anyone hurt you for as long as I live. You are my beloved daughter, my treasure, the star of my sky."

He hugged me and kissed me, then put me back in bed and covered me with a blanket.

"Sleep some more. It's very early."

That was the last time I saw my mother. For the next few years, I also didn't go to any school, but instead the teachers came to me. The lessons lasted over half a day and covered all areas of expertise. I've lost count how many educationalists of both genders have passed through our home. I know that the monthly assessment of my abilities worried my father and uncle Albert, who moved in with us a year after my parents' divorce. Father called one teacher after another an idiot, eventually kicking them out of the house and hiring another in their place. What's obvious, studying in this system, is that I didn't have contact with other children, and I was beginning to feel this isolation from a normal child's world more and more. That's when Silver was born. Although I was not considered particularly smart, I was smart enough to hide his presence from my family and psychologists.

He appeared one rainy day while my father was working on an article for a science newspaper and – as was usually the case – he was drowning in work up to the ears. Uncle Albert left for his company's integration meeting. The house seemed empty without my mother and her noisy friends, who were always present in our lives. I felt more alone than usual, so I took action. I dreamed of an older brother who completely adored me, a brother for whom I was the meaning and content of life. I named him Silvestro Silversnake, or in short – Silver. I don't know how I thought up this name myself. But it seemed fitting for a Mestizo, which he was supposed to be. The photographs in my father's album strongly influenced my imagination, and the programs I later watched on General Geographic inspired my love for Indian culture.

The fact that the Indians were practically gone made me very sad. There were still people on Earth whose genes indicated such heritage, but many, many years ago, the remnants of the Indian tribes left their reservations and mixed in with other races. The professor running the program said that they no longer believed that the persistence in nurturing the remnants of their culture made any sense. The old gentleman's voice sounded very sad. As I understood from the content of the program, he was one of those anthropologists who did not agree with the prevailing theory of omni-populism. I didn't understand it, even though I tried to. After all, what's wrong with different cultures, different groups of people with their own traditions existing on the same planet?

To me it seemed beautiful, but the professor's counter-investigator, a passionate woman with red hair in a short braid, who was slightly younger than him, indignantly resisted his arguments. She reminded of some events in human history, so terrible that I could hardly listen and finally switched the TV to cartoons.

Some things are just not for me, even to this day. I hate descriptions of human misfortunes and catastrophes, even more so the sight of it, so I didn't watch any films aimed at adults, except for light comedies. One day I accidentally switched to a sensational drama and was watching a scene where the main character was stabbed in the side with a knife. I vomited, screamed and cried so hard that father had to give me some medicine to calm me down and sit next to me all night. And I was fifteen at that time.

And that's how a brother appeared in my life, one whom no one could see, not even me. But I was no longer alone. Silver was with me always and everywhere: he bent over me when I hurt my knee, looked over my shoulder while I was painting, and in the evenings he sat next to my bed and told me all kinds of stories. I was generally thought of as stupid, but by that time I was smart enough to hide us from people. Even my father knew nothing about him, let alone the teachers and psychologists who regularly examined me. I was silent about him because I didn't want to lose him. He was too precious to me. Years passed, and I became more and more aware of my loneliness. I didn't go to school, so I didn't have friends.

The neighbors' children didn't visit me or invite me. They were not allowed to by their parents, who thought I was not the right company for their offspring. I myself, after several children threw clods of dirt at me shouting: *Idiot, loser, nobody,* was not too willing to leave the house. It was a terrible experience. I stood there like a statue, not knowing what these children wanted from me, scared and crying, until the kids' parents ran up and dragged them away, telling them that they should be ashamed of such behavior. They made them apologize, but that didn't fix or explain anything, and I ran home crying bitterly. I didn't understand why I was treated this way, and my father didn't want to explain it to me. He only gave me some medicine to calm me down and told me to go to bed early.

So, I was satisfied with our villa and patio for my whole world, as well as the weekend trips with my father and uncle to different fun places. Over time, I got used to it. Then I stopped asking why I didn't go to a regular school like my peers and completely gave up on trying to go out to people. I realized that our house, although large, with two stories, was small in comparison with the street and the city, but I was not bothered by it. I grew up in a voluntary confinement, learning about the outside world only through television and computer communications. I stubbornly watched the scientific channels, and although I sometimes didn't understand much of what was said, I got the impression that through programs about physics, geology, anthropology and botany, I was getting smarter. Finally, I started taking online lessons on a regular basis and found that virtual tutoring didn't give me such panic attacks as live tutors. It even became pleasant to study, and I passionately passed the consecutive levels.

It wasn't because I wanted to be alone. On the contrary, I really wanted human companionship, the best proof of that was my imaginary brother. Although I had enormous problems acquiring knowledge at the school level, I accidentally discovered something that I could learn more than willingly. One of the online educational channels offered dance and stage singing courses from basic to expert. Unbeknownst to my father and uncle Albert, I purchased both of them. I didn't want them to laugh at me, but when I accidentally mentioned it at dinner, they looked at me with unexpected respect.

"Very good, Aurita. Study," said uncle. "I hope you can show us what you've learned, from time to time?"

I blushed to the roots of my hair.

"But of course," I muttered.

Any sign of someone's interest I took as a surprise, even when it came from immediate family members. Maybe it's because – apart from my father and uncle – I knew them very poorly. Sometimes my grandparents came to visit us, but they treated me in a strange way, as if they didn't know what to talk to me about. When they left, I felt relieved. Although I have to admit that they tried. Once they brought my cousins Amador and Itati, but we couldn't find a common tongue. They kept to each other the whole time, and I got the impression that they only knew how to talk to one another. They were wary of me, and, as I understood from what my father told me, they behaved this way towards everyone. It had something to do with their mother, but what it was exactly, no one told me.

Now I was putting even more effort into these lessons. While they worked, I – locked in my room – practiced the instructions coming from the screen on the wall. These were wonderful moments. Once I mastered the basic steps, everything else came on its own. I completed the exercises dictated by the virtual teacher without any problems, and also began to compose my own dances to randomly chosen music. When I got tired of dancing, I picked up the microphone and started singing, watching the reaction of the program. As soon as I started being out of tune, the pulsing lines changed from green to red. It usually took me about a dozen repetition to sing in order for the teacher's avatar on the screen to smile and say: Very good, Aura Maria. Keep it up. Every such praise I received with clapping my hands, feeling joy to the marrow of my bones, as this was only reserved for the students with the best results in the program.

"I always believed in you," my imaginary brother, the handsome green-eyed Mestizo, would say in such cases, touching my shoulder with his brown hand.

I became so familiar with his image that he already became a real person for me. In the evenings, he sat next to me on the bed, and we talked. During the day, he accompanied while I learned dancing and singing, he followed me into the garden, he was present even during the meals, whether I ate alone or not. My father and uncle rarely had breakfast or lunch with me, but we almost always had diner together. It was a great opportunity to talk about the past day and exchange thoughts. Those were the happiest moments, during which I felt that I have some kind of family, besides the hologram teachers, Silver and Rudzia.

The electronic squirrel was still working, perhaps because I took great care of it. Using the diagrams and instructions on the computer, I learned how to clean its circuits and fix whatever was broken. Although reading bored me, especially reading descriptions, I could easily decipher even the most complex pictures. The shortened legend was enough for me to make even the most intricate pattern as bright as the sun. Encouraged by my success with Rudzia, I imported DIY kits from online stores and worked on various things – models of self-propelled robots, mechanical arms that can support this and that, manipulators on extension arms... Father and uncle didn't know about this hobby, but they admired my other hobbies – dancing and singing, which I showed off in my spare time. Yes, they were delighted, and I didn't understand that what I was doing was actually worthless. At that time, I also began to draw, first with pencils, then with charcoal, and finally I started painting.

II

Maybe it wasn't that I didn't attach any importance to the fact that I did not share my life with the right group of peers, which would happen if I went to school or work. It took me a long time to come to terms with it. I treated the subsequent groups of teachers as a necessary evil, not the company I wanted. They usually consisted of four and sometimes three teachers, and each of them diligently hammered into my head something that I didn't understand or cared about. I had no friends that could give me hints or support me, I was alone in the face of the training system.

Over time, I got used to being alone and no longer pondered about the differences of my life the lives of other young people. In the simplicity of my spirit, I felt that I was really no different from others. I was frighteningly naive. A few things should've made me think, such as how the doctors treated me – as if I was still a child. They didn't persuade me to begin my sex life, they did not explain the subtleties associated with my genetic classification, moreover! I didn't even know what it's like. Nobody bothered to tell me about it. I didn't know then that they simply thought of it as a waste of time. I'm sure if I was more interested in social or scientific programs, something would lead me down the right track, but I didn't watch them very often.

The problems began when I was twenty years and six months old. Within one week, we were visited by four officials and a medical commission which examined me very carefully, as if I was a rare specimen. Then the officials took a good look at me, two men and two women. They were dressed alike, in tight-fitting suits, equally well-groomed, sleek as if their hair was plastic. They asked a lot of questions that I couldn't answer most of the time and ordered me to take dozens of tests. I didn't understand what they all meant, and finally I began crying out of fear. This made a very bad impression on the members of the commission. They kept on writing endlessly in their notebooks before they finally got up and left me alone.

"Calm down, dear sister, I'm sure everything will be okay," Silver repeated helplessly, not knowing how to help me. One way or another, for the first time in my life I felt that I was in danger and that nothing could help me. I had never been so terrified before, and the bodyless shadow hanging over me this time could not give me courage. The shouts coming from my father, who was completely furious, did not help. Sitting in the living room, wiping away my tears, I listened to him call the committee members all the worst things. Finally, I kicked off my shoes and crept quietly to the office door where they were talking. The officials tried to calm my father down, and I could hear their voices at times when my father was silent. They said strange things that I didn't quite understand.

"You know the social law," they reasoned. "You've ignored the rules for too long. She is going to be twenty-one soon!"

"She is my daughter!" father shouted. "No one but me has the right to make decisions about her!"

"You are wrong, Mr. Solis, and you are well aware of that. You somehow convinced the board of education, but that couldn't last forever," a female voice explained patiently.

"We understand your affection to your daughter," said another, male voice. "But you have to understand where we're coming from, too. We cannot change legislation just for you. Besides, we do not even have such capabilities. We are contractors, not legislators."

It was quiet for a moment, then I was surprised to hear that my father was crying. I was scared. I have never seen or heard him cry before. I was different, I could afford to cry, but him? The immovable rock of my life? The officials must have felt stupid too. They began saying something so softly that I couldn't make out the words, then they returned to their usual tone.

"We can give you five more months," said one of the men. "Look for a solution, because we don't see one. She is over twenty years old! If she was still a child, perhaps she could've been educated to become a worker and earn money for herself, but it's not possible now. With her IQ, she will be unhappy for the rest of her life, she wouldn't have anyone to talk to even in the workers' colony, because she is too stupid for that. Perhaps if you persist and get to the highest power, they will take pity on you and give her a small social pension, or she will remain in your sole custody, in both cases alone and without prospects. We must not allow that to happen. Society today cannot afford to support the worthless and outcasts, all the more since, under the right circumstances, they can become dangerous to public order."

"I don't think you have any human feelings at all," father said bitterly.

"That is not true," one of the employees objected. "We do have them. We think about everything."

"We should give you a referral to test your levels of monoamine oxidase[1]," the doctor who examined me entered the conversation. "You have clear symptoms of deficiency and that may explain your behavior.".

"Can't you people understand that I just love my daughter?!" father shouted in despair. "Don't take her away from me! You can't! It's not fair…"

The officials and doctors talked for a while in a low whisper, then one of them said:

"You have five months. Maybe you can find a way. As for our part, all we can promise is that we will not bother you until the end of this period. The whole situation is so abnormal that it justifies the application of the third amendment to the rules."

At these words, my father exploded with rage again and ordered his guests to leave. I bounced off the door and hid behind a decorative coat hanger so that they wouldn't see me. I was more

---

[1] An enzyme, deficiency of which leads to mood disorders.

scared than ever and still didn't understand anything. What were these people trying to do to me? Is my father not able to protect me? What did I even do wrong that the officials became interested? After all, I hardly even left the house, except when Uncle Albert and father took me somewhere – to an amusement park, to a park in a remote area, or to a videoart zoo. I can't remember doing anything reprehensible on these trips. I tried to call in Silver with my thoughts, but somehow, as if to spite me, he disappeared somewhere. I felt alone like never before.

Waiting for the door to close behind the commission, I left my hiding place and ran into the living room. My father was sitting at the table with his head in his hands and crying, and Uncle Albert was standing next to him. He must have been present during the conversation with the officials, but he was silent all the time, as if he didn't want to or could not say anything.

"Come in, Aura Maria," he said when he saw me, "we need to talk. We've delayed this conversation for far too long anyway."

Father raised his head and wiped his face with a handkerchief. He breathed heavily for a moment, as if he still couldn't calm down, then waved his hand at me.

"Sit down, Aurita," he said. "Albert is right, we need to talk."

I obediently sat down in the soft chair opposite him and clasped my hands in my lap. I felt like a convict before an execution, although I still couldn't understand what crime I had committed.

"We live in a well-organized world," father began. "Everything has its place, and the rules determine what we are allowed to do.

The legislators who built our civilization after the Great Ecological Disaster were concerned about humanity's safety, but most of all they had in mind the public good. Therefore, they decided that not everyone should have the right to have children, and not all children should develop. They've also introduced a caste system, the division of people according to their level of intelligence. Each was required to perform a job appropriate to their abilities and innate IQ. Initially, representatives of certain castes were marked with a corresponding symbol on their forehead, which was abandoned later. However, what survived was the practice of separating different social layers from each other, for their own good. Because just think about it, what can a doctor and a scientist have in common? They don't make the right company for each other. For their own good, they must be in separate circles of society. This is why the working class today lives in separate areas, where nobody lacks anything for happiness, but where none of the upper classes settle. It's for the better. At least that's what I've always thought..."

"And now you don't think so anymore?" I dared to ask. He shook his head.

"I have no idea. You see, it was completely different before. In the old world, no one would be bothering us. Society was mixed, people multiplied as they wanted and with whom they wanted. There were many who were crippled, often from birth. People who could work had to donate part of their wages to support people with disabilities. Not only those who, you know, suffered from some kind of an accident, but also those who were born unsuitable for life and ended up in special institutions or were cared for by their families. When the ecological disaster began, food became so scarce that rationing was introduced, and at the same time the law was changed. It became very restrictive in that aspect."

I tried to imagine these changes, but my imagination put forth such terrible images, that I quickly tried to clear my mind of them.

"And people simply agreed to such restrictions of their freedom?"

Father smiled bitterly.

"People were so terrified and tired of the whole situation that they were begging for strong leadership that would carry out social reforms. They didn't protest anything. Curfew, prison camps, equal sentencing regardless of the offender's age... the issue of reproduction was the most controversial, but they managed with that, too. Today, the right to have a child is a privilege available only to people tested for social aptitude. Adequate IQ, genes without defects that could lead to diseases of offspring, psychological structure... it's a whole, highly developed branch of science called neatocreatiology. It's to ensure that the next generation is healthy, strong and intelligent. And so that society doesn't waste resources on providing for useless people who will remain so until the end of their days. However, sometimes it's impossible to predict everything while the child is still in the womb or immediately after birth. The child develops, and then, only a few years later does it turn out that they are significantly different from their peers. That's when they are taken to the workers' estate, where they are trained to become an operator of simple machines. It's best for everyone," he paused to catch his breath. "Everyone learns about this, and is of the same opinion. I did too, until it turned out that my own daughter was a little... different."

"Different?" I repeated. "Why am I *different*?"

He stroked his hair nervously.

"Do you remember how it was back at school?" he asked. "And what the teachers at home were saying later on? When you were born, doctors said that your intellectual development was difficult to predict. The older you became, the more obvious it was that you stood out from the other children, but we still hoped to fix that somehow. Then you got sick... maybe I made a mistake, because I allowed you to grow up not knowing that you don't fit into society. Your mother was probably right, because if we transferred you to the adaptation center for future workers, you would probably be living a relatively normal life by now. But I couldn't... I couldn't..."

"Dad..."

"Don't say anything for now. I was hoping that if I hired the best specialists, they would find a way to prove that you are useful in our class. But that didn't work. As they said, you are a child in the body of an adult woman, and it will remain so."

"If we were living in a different era, your artistic talent could have helped," said Uncle Albert. "You are a great dancer; you sing like an angel. You can paint and draw. It's just that today there are no live dancers or singers, even actors, their roles are substituted by correctly programmed holograms. As for drawing, the only ones that count are technical ones, since we have so many artificial methods for reproducing reality or obtaining an abstract image.

You are like a wildflower completely useless for the public good. The fact that we both love you very much doesn't matter to the officials."

I got up.

"What are they going to do to me?" I whispered. My uncle came over and hugged me protectively.

"Calm down, Aurita. You still have us, and we will fight for you."

"They want to take you to an institution for low-developed people for a final diagnosis and... decision," father said. "I thought that, as long as I live, nobody will insist on that, but some overzealous official from the school board sniffed out your files. He filled out the appropriate forms, and the case was sent to the higher ups. Then there was a lot of fuss. Your mother foresaw it all, she wanted to get it over with while you were still little, and end it, but I didn't agree... I believed that I could do... a miracle."

"We really need one now," uncle added. "You may be in danger for euthanasia as a potentially dangerous entity, since you don't fit in anywhere."

"How am I bothering them?" I said, completely in tears.

I couldn't understand what these people wanted. After all, I haven't done anything bad, I don't even leave the house! Why do they want to take me to some 'institution' and subject me to 'euthanasia'? And what does that word even mean? Now I regretted that I didn't watch the social programs, and it dawned on me that I really didn't know anything about the world around me. I didn't like to learn what I was told to, I was bored with mathematics, chemistry, geography, history, literature... why was I told to read such boring books as The *Naked and the Dead* when there are so many interesting subjects in the digital library available on the Internet? Why do I need to know what regions Australia is divided into? I won't go there anyway. And information such as *human body contains atoms to the power of ten to twenty-eighth* was completely abstract to me. Who counted them and for what purpose? Either way, sure, they do, so what? Or that some king had his head cut off a long time ago... oh, this I didn't want to read or hear at all!

I hated the bloody and violent stories from the old days. After all, they are all over, we have to forget about them. I didn't want to know any of them. The only thing that interested me was drawing, singing and dancing, which I was passionately engaged in. I loved beauty. Flowers, music, paintings... was it all a crime against society?

I raised my tearful eyes towards my father. He was still sitting in the chair, his handsome face seemed old and tired. He always looked like the most attractive man in the world to me, although, if I was being honest, I have met very few of them in person. Announcers, actors, maybe holograms, but still indistinguishable from living people on the screen, were no match for him. Tall, broad-shouldered, with dark skin, curly brown hair and very beautiful eyes, light gray, like pebbles in a pond. He was like an idol for me. For the first time, I realized that, contrary to my belief, he is not omnipotent.

"Aura Maria, we will not surrender," he said slowly, decisively. "I will find a way to save you, even if I have to fight the whole world. I won't let them waste you. I said this to your mother when she was leaving, and I'm saying it again now. Don't cry anymore, because my heart can't take it!

I quickly wiped away my tears, took a deep breath, closed my eyes and summoned Silver. I imagined him standing next to me in a black leather jacket over his bare body, tall, thin, with straight hair running down his back. His chiseled face was motionless, his green eyes glistening. Thanks to him, I will never be alone, even in the *institution,* whatever that place may be.

III

My sense of security was gone. Despite the fact that I was promised five months of peace, when I heard the doorbell I hid in the corner, I couldn't eat during the day or sleep at night. I lost weight, I developed dark circles under my eyes, and I completely neglected my daily exercises. I spent my entire days sitting in the courtyard with Rudzia on my lap, staring blankly at the bushes of Chinese roses. I didn't even watch the TV. I was afraid and had the feeling of being persecuted, although my father and uncle did everything, they could to distract me from it. I stared with fear at the calendar, counting the days. I was given five months, that is, until I turned twenty-one, the limit beyond which a modern person should already be completely independent, because that is the law.

One day I forced myself to search the Internet for information about the asylum for the dependent, but there was little public information available. I only learned that this is a therapy center and that non-predictive cases are put into euthanasia. I didn't understand this last word until I looked in the dictionary. When I finally put it all together, I understood my father's violent reaction. But I, myself – surprisingly – calmed down. I realized that my fear was mainly caused by the fact that I didn't know what exactly was waiting for me. Now I knew. I should have been twice as afraid, because although I didn't yet know whether I would be non-predictive, I was in danger of lethal injection. And yet I was no longer afraid. I realized that my father would in fact do everything to save me from being sent to the institution, and I felt a surge of confidence. After all, if he was able to get me home schooling and a special 'card' from the school board, it meant that he never gives up.

Looking through the Internet, I learned that the *special treatment card* is issued very rarely, in cases examined individually. Holders of such a card received education only at home, from their parents and their chosen teachers. They had time until the age of twenty-one to become useful members of society. If they were unable to do so, they would be sent to an orphanage, and that is what happened to me. Now I had a better understanding of what the many teams of teachers were doing at our home. Each of them tried to educate me in a different direction, and in the end they all gave up. Was I that useless?

I opened my personal locker and pulled out my recently purchased camera drone kit. I haven't finished it yet. I suppose the question is why I didn't show these toys to my father. Well, they were mainly meant for kids and their purpose was to teach manual skills. The more advanced ones, the ones I've been importing for a year or so, were usually bought by groups of young technicians and served them in interclub competitions. I didn't belong to any of them and thought they were more suitable for boys, so I was ashamed of my passion. Was that stupid? Maybe, but that's what I thought, and as proud as I was of my dancing and singing, willingly showing off to my father and uncle, my passion for DIY seemed out of place. Years later, I remembered how one day my mother took away the educational toy that my uncle Albert had bought for me.

"That's more suitable for boys, isn't it!" she said indignantly. The toy was a simple hand-made mechanism, and I was about five years old then. This incident must have been etched in my memory and convinced me that there is a division in the world between what is right for women and what is for men. This assumption is fundamentally wrong, but it is still prevalent in some families. My mother probably belonged to one of them. Perhaps her reaction was also influenced by the fact that she didn't like uncle.

Sometimes, when I think about it, I painfully realize how little I know of her. All I have is one small holopic. In it, I see a tall red-haired woman with a keen gaze and a face that resembles an impersonal beauty from a fashion site. This sight doesn't arise any emotions in me. I don't think I loved her, and she didn't love me. Even when she was at home, she rarely cared for me. Did she want to be a mother at all? She might have wanted to, but she certainly didn't expect a daughter like me. Maybe after leaving father, she married another man, and I have half-brothers and sisters, whom I know nothing about? These were rather sad thoughts, especially since I won't find the answer to them.

*****

Time passed, and one day uncle Albert burst into the house, excited as never before. His angular, expressive face radiated with such a smile that it became almost beautiful, even though uncle was never considered a handsome man.

"I found the answer!" he shouted.

My father jumped up from the table at which we were playing *Ludo*. His excitement reflected on me too, although I didn't understand what it was about. Uncle put a folded piece of paper on the table. I looked at it with my mouth open. I knew that paper was still in use, but only occasionally, for example, to print a diploma or a wedding invitation on it. Documents were sent in electronic form, sometimes computer foil was used, which, however, was gradually replaced by *pods*. There was also paperboard, although plastic, but almost indistinguishable from wood pulp. I ordered it myself for drawing. But I've never seen... a printout from a computer beofre, except for one of the TV shows where they showcased it. Nowadays, paper is too valuable to waste on printouts, which is why I was so surprised. I didn't even dare to touch the thin, almost transparent sheet of paper. My father was the one who did so.

"So, it's true," he said after a long pause as he moved his eyes through it several times. "We found an exit from our labyrinth."

"What do you mean?" I asked helplessly.

He looked at me. His eyes were shining, his lips trembling slightly, and I had the feeling that I was looking at someone who achieved enlightenment a moment ago.

"Aura Maria..." he said and only then inhaled sharply, as if he was about to dive into water. "You will face a difficult test, but I believe that you can handle it. As you know, all this time, since the state commission paid us a visit, we have been looking for some way to help you. We didn't find it on Earth, so I got the idea to look higher up."

"What do you mean *higher up*?"

Father sat down. I saw that it was difficult for him to overcome the urge to bring me to his knees, as he did when I was younger, when he had something important to tell me.

"I don't know if you've heard of the only extraterrestrial settlement so far," he began. "It's on the planet Patris, with which the Earth is in constant contact. It was created relatively recently, about ten years ago. One of the first colonists was my sister and our two younger brothers. I managed to establish contact with them. Nando and Diogo, are of course adults by now, although I remember them only as the mischievous little bastards, whom were always everywhere. In any case, they answered my letter and are ready to take care of you."

My head was spinning. An extraterrestrial settlement? I was not interested in space and the history of astronautics, of course I knew about scientific orbital stations and industrial cities on the lunar surface, but they didn't interest me. I also never thought about leaving our planet. This idea struck me as completely absurd, and that must have been clear to see, because uncle Albert joined my father.

"My friend from college, Mickey Livigst. is now an inspector at the Space Center," he explained. "It was he who allowed us contact with Patris, because not everyone has such privilege, of course. It was also important to send the message without it being censored, so he worked hard before figuring that out for us. That's why he made a printout. The original recording had to be quickly erased so that it did not fall into the wrong hands. He risked a lot..."

"Let's get to the point," father interrupted him. "This week *Hyamdal* will take off, a cargo rocket with equipment for settlers. There will also be hibernation capsules on board. In fact, these types of ships usually do not carry colonists, but this is an exception. Several families with children and a small detachment of soldiers are flying with it. One of the passengers was also supposed to be Kendra Wilson, a planetologist. However, it turned out that the girl is pregnant, so she must stay on Earth. Lighting technician Alma Jablonsky was supposed to replace her, but she changed her mind and now refuses to go. Since such an argument will surely not be accepted by her superiors, she wants to evade flight in a very legal way, that is, substituting someone in her place. Mickey already had a candidate for her place, but didn't have time to notify her. Luckily for us... In short, you are taking her place."

I nearly fainted. I must have turned very pale because my father and uncle were visibly frightened. They started fanning me, my uncle even brought a glass of water and sprinkled it in my face.

"Calm down, Aurita!" he exclaimed. "You won't be alone there... Johnny, tell her something! After all, it's not a juvenile camp, but a beautiful place, filled with greenery! No one will hurt you there, they will take care of you.

"It's true," father backed him up vehemently. "My sister will take good care of you. Poor Etta... I was so unfair to her. Now I understand how she felt when I demanded that she moves out."

"Why did you do that, dad?" I looked at him with big eyes.

"The Santis family, your maternal grandparents, were very conservative. The news that the sister of the future son-in-law was genetically useless could have discouraged them, and then Carmen Antonia wouldn't have married me. She was very dominated by her parents," he took a deep breath. "Sometimes I get the feeling that what happened to me is a punishment imposed onto me by the ancient gods for my insensitivity and selfishness."

"Johnny..." uncle said warningly.

Father shrugged his shoulders.

"No one else is here. I've studied history for so long that sometimes I unintentionally treat Taranis or Isis as a real supernatural force. Anyway, back to Etta."

He opened the closet and took out a holoalbum. He flipped through a few items, then pressed the button next to the selected photo. Above the album appeared a three-dimensional portrait of him and a slender blonde with neatly combed locks into a hairstyle fashionable some twenty years ago. I knew immediately that this must have been Aunt Estrella, whom I have never seen before. Her resemblance to my father left no doubts. The same neat nose, a beautifully outlined chin and the same gray eyes in the shape of oblong leaves. Although she seemed much smaller than her brother, whose height measured nearly two meters, with a proportionate physique. The second hologram showed two boys, playing badminton, who looked like two peas in a pod.

"Is that Diogo and Nando?" I asked.

"Father nodded."

"They are about ten years old here. I don't even know what they look like now. Etta has genetic predisposition of group zero, she is not allowed to have children of her own, so the family has always treated her like the fifth wheel in a cart. But not these two."

"And what is my group?" I looked inquiringly at my father.

He rubbed his hand on his cheek in a confusion I couldn't understand.

"You were assigned group two at birth, but right now you still won't be allowed to have a child," he said reluctantly. "All the tests are taken into account, including psychological tests and IQ scores. Eh, that's not the point now!"

"Why?" I stamped my foot in sudden anger. "You say that I am a child in a woman's body, but whose fault is that? You never talk to me seriously! Now at least explain to me why I'm not allowed to have my own little girl! Because maybe I would like to have one!"

Uncle Albert suppressed a nervous laugh that escaped him at these words.

"Excuse me. Johnny, she's right. We have always tried to protect her at all costs. And we did that even too well. The girl grew up under a lampshade, knowing little about the modern world and its pitfalls. This was partly out of necessity because she was unable to attend regular school after she became sick, but we were also overly protective. And what came of it?"

Father nodded. His excitement subsided, he was tired and looked as if he suddenly aged. He looked at least ten years older than my uncle, even though I knew he was older than my father. I didn't pay attention to it then, but today I know that Uncle Albert took great care of himself. He not only dressed like a young person, but also regularly used the services of beauty salons, thanks to which an outsider could easily assume he is about twenty-five to thirty years old. It was strange, but I still don't know what kind of family connection we've had. We didn't talk about it at home, and I didn't ask about it. He was my uncle, and that's all I knew. However, he was not in any of the photographs in the holoalbum. Why? Only now am I starting to think about it, when there's no longer anyone who could answer my question.

"Nothing good," he said. "It's our fault that Aurita is lonely and unable to function in society. Truth be told, I feel that Carmen Antonia had some right in what she said. If she had been sent to an adaptation center then, she would have been working in some kind of production today and would have been quite happy. She would have acquaintances, friends, maybe even... a boyfriend? She is so pretty after all."

I felt myself blushing. I didn't consider myself a great beauty, although I knew I wasn't ugly. I would have to be extremely stupid to know that. Yes, I am pretty. I have my mother's wide, slightly slanted eyes, green like fresh grass, figure, and round face. A classic nose after my father. Although from where I got my tawny skin, hair so dark that they looked dark blue, and my lips of a cherry color... I could only guess. Could it be that my keen interest in the Indians stems from my genetic memory? Who knows? I once saw Aunt Naela's holographic sister, the second of my father's sisters, who was in an asylum for the mentally ill. Only her family had dark skin and dark hair, though not as black as mine, but rather straight. Mine, by its very nature, swirls like my father's and creates heavy waves.

Could I have been popular among young men if it weren't for my pitiful IQ? I thought about it for the first time. As I learned later, in addition to vitamins, I was given medications prescribed by a doctor to blocking my hormonal system in such a way that I would not feel any sexual attraction at all. This the education board's condition, which allowed individual training and education up to age 21. I think they recently stopped giving them to me because I have grown more interested in films in which people express their love towards each other. I used to think that they were stupid and uninteresting, now I liked looking at them, and often, before falling asleep, I dreamed that I was the heroine of one of them.

"But... I'm happy with you," I muttered, embarrassed.

Uncle stroked my head like a little child.

"We won't be here forever, and in addition, official factors intervened in our affairs, which we tried our best to avoid," he said seriously. "You have to find your own piece of the world and I think this colony is a good idea. Mickey told me about it. Life there is a little different than on Earth, and according to slightly different rules. I don't know all the details, but I heard that the colonists are worried about earthly authorities. Obviously, they don't follow the rules of genetic purity properly. You know, it's hard to control this many people over billions of miles. There, new social connections are formed and new laws are created that are adapted to conditions different from Earth," for a moment he paused. He must have felt some uncertainty in his voice, and the words unconvincing. "I'm not going to deceive you, Aurita, I myself don't know what it's like there. Johnny simply informed the brothers about your situation in a short message, and they answered..." he took a second print from his pocket. "Dear brother, Aura Maria will be safe here, we will find a job for her and no one will hurt her. If you figure out how to send her to us, we'll take care of the rest."

My expression probably didn't exude excitement, because my father hastily added:

"This doesn't mean that you will rely only on them. Albert and I already have a plan. The ship with another group of colonists will start in six months. Recently, interest in migration to Patris has dropped significantly, as it turned out that the disasters predicted by scientists will pass close to us. We'll get in easily. You'll see, everything will be fine."

I hardly listened to him, afraid of what awaited me. I rarely even left the house, never alone. As a child, I was outside my hometown only once in my life. And now I had to leave my home planet forever and go to an extraterrestrial colony!

"I don't want to," I whispered.

"Unfortunately, you have no choice. Things have gone too far at this point," my uncle decided to lay out his cards on the table in simple and rude language. "Aurita, you are already suitable for euthanasia as a person incapable of social adaptation. Do you understand? We won't keep beating ourselves in the chest and repeating that it's all our fault, because that's pointless. We have to save you, and that's what we're doing!"

I swallowed my tears with effort. I had to overcome my hysteria; it wouldn't help anything. He must have been right. I thought that I didn't want to die at all, and that the law was cruel if it wants to force me to. How am I bothering anyone?

I couldn't sleep that night. Silver sat next to me on the bed and was silent. For the first time, he was unable to cheer me up or help me, although I could still feel his comforting presence. I have the impression that it was on that very night that I quickly grew from a spoiled child to a young woman frightened of life.

IV

The first thing I remember after waking up from hibernation was nausea. Then my hearing returned to me – mixed sounds, creating an unbearable cacophony. I couldn't cover my ears because I couldn't control my body. After a very long time, the sounds began to line up in familiar configurations and ceased to annoy me. My memory returned, and the images filled one after another.

My father woke me up in the middle of the night.

"Get dressed, Aurita," he whispered. "Albert was able to arrange transport for us. He succeeded at the last moment. We must be at the launch site before dawn, otherwise everything will be lost."

I was ready in five minutes. The clothes I was supposed to wear on the day of my escape have been sitting ready on the chair for almost a week, all I had to do was reach for them.

My father took me out of the house through the back door. Outside, a car was waiting – an official limousine for private use, provided only public service officials, and those of the highest rank. Where did Uncle Albert get it from?

Huddled in the back seat, I was shaking like a leaf in the wind. I have never ridden in a personal vehicle before, moreover, driven by a person, and not by a computer connected to a local control network. Until now, I had no idea that such a primitive action was still possible, but now I realized that it had to be. At any stage of development, people could not completely surrender to artificial intelligence, it would be too dangerous. Even I knew that this would lead to a dangerous stagnation and, as a consequence, to the degeneration of humanity.

We must have been driving at the highest allowed speed, because at times it pressed me into the chair. The car did not emit any lights, although according to the rules, it should. I assumed it was part of the disguise, after all, our journey had to be kept secret for the plan to succeed. I didn't know what tricks Uncle Albert was using, but they must have been good, as only after we crossed half the distance did the rearview camera screen show a shape that followed our trail. It was also an individual vehicle, but larger than ours, and the flashing of sensors on the control panel indicated that our uninvited companion was armed. After a few moments, a series of lights flashed above us – two short and one long. The police night code which meant *Stop for Inspection*. They don't use sirens for this at night.

"They found us," my father said. His voice was as calm as ever, as if we weren't in any danger.

"I can see that," Uncle Albert looked completely indifferent. "Hold onto something, it'll shake us a little. Johnny, get ready and open my side window as soon as we turn."

My father put his finger on the touch button and tightened the seat belt with his other hand.

I grabbed the back of the chair. The car, driven by my uncle's hand, accelerated, then turned abruptly into a corner, and uncle threw something out the open window so quickly that I barely had time to notice the movement. Then we drove away, getting back to the previous route at an arc.

"What was that?" I asked weakly.

"A holographic projector," he replied. "It'll confuse them long enough for us to get away."

Not too convinced, I did not take my eyes off the rearview camera screen, but apart from trucks and public transport vehicles, I didn't notice anything else. Soon we arrived at the cosmodrome. My father slipped a disc with an access code into the emitter of our limo – as I noticed, it probably differed from a typical recording medium in its manufacture material. It was not a standard gray, but a pale gold, which signified strict encoding. I didn't even want to think about how my uncle got it.

The codes must have been actual, as all the gates opened in front of us without triggering an alarm. Before the last one, a young man in the uniform of technical service was waiting for us, shifting from foot to foot and looking around the entire time.

"Is that her?" he asked nervously when I exited the vehicle. "To be honest, if it were not for my debts, I wouldn't have taken such risks..."

"All right, all right," father interrupted him. He pulled out a card from his wallet. "As we agreed. This is Alma Jablonsky, she changed her mind at the last minute and you saw no reason not to let her on board as she is still on the list. You're covered, as long as you keep your mouth shut."

The technician hid the card with ill-concealed zeal. Uncle got my suitcases out of the trunk.

"Quickly, Johnny. We have to get back on the road. No one can link our night trip to the spaceport."

I desperately grabbed my father's hand. He freed himself firmly but carefully.

"Calm down, Aurita. Remember what we talked about. This is just a temporary goodbye."

He kissed me and got into the car, which drove away silently into the night.

A temporary goodbye... now I know he was lying.

The technician didn't give me time to cry. He pushed me with my suitcases into the melex and lead me under the body of the ferry, which was darkening in the distance, which was supposed to transport the hibernation capsules to the destination ship. He led me inside along the still lowered ladder and, shining a flashlight into a dark room, led me into the hold. There were a dozen closed pods, with flashing LEDs, and one that was open.

"Please take off your clothes and get inside. Hands along your body," he ordered me sharply.

"Strip nude? In front of you?" my eyes widened.

"Yes, nude, what's wrong with you? And take of all jewelry too, if you have any," he snorted impatiently. "I can turn around. What a joke, I've seen more naked boobs than you have flowers in the garden. It's no attraction."

Overcoming my embarrassment, I took off my jumpsuit, shoes and underwear, removed the hairpins from my hair and, as he told me, sank into the foamy inside of the capsule.

"Close your eyes and breathe calmly," the man gathered my clothes and put them in a bag next to the capsule, which I had not noticed before. "Don't be afraid. You will not feel anything but the scent of jasmine. This is the hibernation gas. Then you will fall asleep. I wish you a happy awakening."

The last thing I heard was the click of the closing lid.

******

I began to feel my body and my vision slowly returned to me. At first there was just fog, then blurry spots, then more and more clear outlines. I was in some kind of big doctor's office. They took my blood, took pictures and asked many questions. On many of them I did not know how to answer correctly, they said that this was the result of confusion after hibernation, and that it would disappear later. There were other passengers nearby, awakening from hibernation. They were examined in the same way as me, with many notes about the results being written. All of them must have felt as terrible as I have, because they were pale and exhausted. Two women and one man vomited; the children were crying loudly. This really irritated me, and in the end, I could barely keep myself from screaming, and yet I had to lie down here for several days. First, they gave me a lot of drip-bags, then they repeated the tests, and finally, they gave me a shot with multivaccine, after which I was vomiting for the next two days and had a fever.

I breathed a sigh of relief when I was finally discharged from the medical facility and told to go to the office. The young, well-built man in a khaki uniform who sat there handed me a pod.

"Read this and sign," he said cheerfully. He looked at me with clear pleasure. "And put your thumb here. Good. Now they will put a monitoring bracelet on your ankle."

"What for?" I asked, scared.

"Standard procedure. Each visitor is monitored for a month to identify any problems," he said quickly and soothingly. Leaning over, he fixed a metal strip with glowing LEDs on my ankle. "If all readings are good, in a month it will open and fall off by itself."

The prospect of constant surveillance was frustrating, but ultimately what was I supposed to do? I must have had an unclear expression, because the clerk quickly added:

"You won't even feel it. Everyone has to go through this. Please sign the protocol. Good. Now I will bring you your luggage. Please take it and go to the starting station. The shuttle will take you all to the city."

The *pod* contained my data, the real data, not the one that allowed me to get into the hibernation capsule and aboard the ship. This should have given me food for thought, but I was too weak for that. I signed it at the indicated place and handed it to the clerk. He hid it, then got up and brought two suitcases from the back room. He put them in front of me. All the while, he didn't take his eyes off of me. I think he liked me, even though I was pale, disheveled and exhausted. At the same time, I didn't feel afraid of the new place, but probably only because I still didn't have the strength to be. The suitcases placed on a small, flat cart were everything I've brought from Earth, packed by my father and uncle, not even by me. If I hadn't been haunted by nausea, I probably would have cried out at the sight of them, they reminded me so much of the lost home. So, I grabbed the handle of the trolley and trudged to the square where the shuttle was waiting. It was already half full, but we still had to wait.

I sat down in the chair pointed to me and closed my eyes, trying my best to imagine that I was on Earth. Then I tried to summon Silver, but this was the first time I failed. I thought it was probably due to the presence of all these people, shuffling their feet, coughing, talking... several children were crying, the girl kept saying: "But I want to pee!" to the point that I wanted to get up and throw her out the door. Maybe I would have done it, but looking back at her, I finally saw that the little girl was impatiently picking her nose with her fingers, which her mother ignored, and I felt sick. The transport nurse handed me a waterproof bag and held my head.

"Relax, it happens after hibernation," she said soothingly and after a while brought me a tiny pill. "Please swallow it and breathe some pure oxygen for a moment. Here, from this mask."

I put the plastic triangle connected with a thick wire to my mouth. I don't know why I reacted so violently. I've always been overly sensitive, but I could keep myself in control. Now I could see that I was acting like a jelly and I was ashamed of myself. It was another new feeling that I experienced for the first time in my life – I mean, I were embarrassed before for different reason, but not because I'm reacting to different situations like a child. I never had any reason to be ashamed of this, because back at home they've made all the efforts so that I didn't have to feel and act like an adult. After all, my father tried to keep me as a child, keep me from growing up.

Now I could see that others don't behave this way, and decided that I needed to adjust, no matter how difficult it was. In the meantime, I inhaled long gulps of oxygen, slowly suppressing the nausea. With that in mind, I didn't even notice as the shuttle jerked and lifted into the air.

The flight was short and fast, and when the ship's door opened again, I saw the landing pad and people gathered behind the barrier. Some held banners with names written on them, others held large bouquets of flowers. I could see even from far away that these were fresh flowers, and the amazement made me dizzy. Each such bouquet on Earth would cost the equivalent of the average official's weekly salary. Once I watched a program on the Nature channel, where they showed a price list for flowers grown for the needs of green centers. Wild plants were not allowed to be picked or even touched, and severe penalties were imposed for this. It really must have been different here.

I walked slowly down the ladder, dragging my suitcases with me. Looking around, I finally saw the badge raised high with the words *Aura Maria Solis*, and without enthusiasm headed in the same direction. I expected to see two middle-aged men and a woman, but to my surprise, a girl of about fifteen was holding the badge on a long stand. Next to her stood a handsome blond man with freckles on his cheeks and a dark-haired, dark-skinned woman with ears formed in the spitz, which was already out of fashion on Earth. I didn't recognize any of them, but I noticed a distant resemblance to my father in the teenager. I stopped, detonated.

"I am Aura Maria..." I said uncertainly. The girl wrinkled her nose, smiled broadly and took my hand.

"Hi, aunt," she exclaimed, shaking my hand enthusiastically. "I was so curious how you look like. I'm Jamie, well, actually Gemma Solis-Willner, but everyone calls me Jamie. Estrella Solis was my mother."

"Mother? But she was a zero..."

"We'll explain everything, but not here," the blonde intervened. "Allow me to introduce myself: Kenneth Linde, supervisor of the local hospital and the legal guardian of this kid. And this Iieutenant Tina Roberts, our chief of police, and my wife. Let's go to our car."

"What do you mean legal guardian, why?" I asked, confused.

"My mom died when I was five," Jamie told me lightly. "I hardly remember her. Dad Ken and Mom Tina took care of me. Do you know that I was the first child born on this planet?"

Etta died... I don't know why, but my heart ached. I didn't know this woman, I saw only her image, but somehow, I felt that she was close to me. Dr. Linde elbowed the girl under the shoulder blade lightly, and my eyes involuntarily widened. On Earth, it was forbidden to hit anyone, even in jest, only light tapping with an open palm was allowed.

"You were the first, but only from our group," he said reproachingly. "Don't mislead your aunt. Aura Maria, your luggage please."

Several dozen, strange looking, small cars were parked in the large square. They were not at all like the cars popular on Earth. First of all, their undersides were equipped with wheels, not sleds, and their roofs looked very strange. As I got closer, I realized they were just solar panels that could be tilted or adjusted to the sun as needed. The local cars didn't need fuel, so they were only used for short distances. The exact characteristics of these types of panels were unknown to me, but my father once told me that this is a bad way to charge larger batteries. Light scattering and a few other factors that I didn't understand are involved. However, as long as you don't travel long distances, it is cost effective and environmentally friendly.

"Our car is over there," Tina Roberts pointed to one of the cars. Coming closer, I saw a young man in gray overalls sitting behind the primitive control console. When I approached, he turned his head towards me. He had an incredibly calm, somewhat absent expression on his face, regular features and long, warm brown eyes. He looked at me with neither curiosity, nor kindness, nor reluctance. It took a while to understand what I saw in those beautiful eyes: it was nothing. Nothing at all. No emotions, just a reflection of the surrounding world. He saw my existence and accepted it, nothing more. Was he not attracted to me? Or maybe he wasn't attracted to women at all?

I was usually afraid of strangers. True, I had nothing to do with them before. However, now, driven by an incomprehensible whim, I suddenly wanted to attract the attention of this handsome boy with black hair and delicate eyes. Maybe because he was so in line with my imagined ideal... well, I don't know... lover? I didn't even realize what the word meant. The ideal object of attraction, let's say. I held out my hand.

"Hi there. I am Aura Maria Solis."

Slowly, as if hesitantly, he took my hand. His skin was smooth as silk and surprisingly cool.

"Raul," he said, and then added, "Raul 209C."

I heard Jamie laughing loudly behind me. She patted me on the shoulder.

"Auntie, that's just a robot!" she exclaimed.

I was dumbfounded. A robot? I've seen robots on Earth, and they looked completely different. I looked around to see Kenneth stuffing my luggage in a box behind the car.

"Jamie, please," he said irritably. "Raul is an android, not a robot. You might as well call a laser cutter a chisel."

The girl wrinkled her nose and shrugged, which probably meant she had an opinion on the matter, and probably on every other topic as well.

"Forgive her, my dear," said Tina Roberts. "She's in a difficult age and has a difficult character. Get in. You can sit in front if you'd like."

I obeyed her, more and more dazed. I had a headache from an excess of sensations, and I didn't know how to react now. I felt terribly stupid, especially since I still couldn't help but look at Raul. The realization that this is a product of advanced technology made me not disgusted, but rather curious. I knew that androids think independently and therefore should be treated like living beings, not like things – I once watched programs on this topic. However, I have never interacted with AI myself and didn't understand what such an advanced android is doing in this colony.

Jamie must have guessed what I was thinking, because as the weird-looking van pulled out of the landing zone, she slapped me on the shoulder.

"Aunt, may I call you by name?" she chirped and, without waiting for an answer, continued. "I see that Raul has picked your curiosity. He belonged to my mother. She really liked him. He took care of me when I was little and still keeps trying to, which can be damn annoying."

"Jamie..." Linda protested weakly. She ignored it.

"It didn't bother me when I was little, but now, oh! He may not be too assertive, but he tries to follow me as if I still need supervision. It can be quite enraging. No privacy."

"Stop it! He's not a vacuum cleaner, but an android, and he can hear you!" the doctor raised his voice threateningly. Instinctively, I curled up in my chair. The talkative kid didn't even pay attention to it.

"So, what if he can? After all, he has no feelings."

"Your late mother thought differently. And she really liked him."

"Oh, I was curious when you would start with that. My mother was a terrible idealist and believed in everything. She dressed him in fashionable clothes, asked what he thought, they even slept together. I, on the other hand, am a realist, and I will not treat a robot like a human being, because that's just complete idiocy."

I glanced furtively at Raul. His clean profile remained motionless, as if he heard nothing. I knew what he was now, but somehow, I still felt bad for him hearing such things. Jamie should be less eccentric in his presence. To hide my embarrassment, I began to look around.

The view was extraordinary and incredibly beautiful. Patris gave me the impression of a gigantic nature reserve, and I involuntarily wondered if we were allowed to be here. On Earth, it was forbidden and very severely punished, but here everything was different. The surrounding greenery practically boiled with dozens of hues, the sounds of insect and animal activity came from all around, and the sky was deep blue-purple with occasional silver clouds. They looked like they were painted with light polish of the Light Mirror brand – mirrored sails illuminated by the rays of the small sun. I looked at them as if entranced, until I was startled by a huge shape that glided high above our heads. It looked like a wavy shade, under which twisted thin cords stretched. Illuminated by the sun's rays, it shimmered pink, juicy red and dark purple.

"What is that?!" I shouted in fright, pointing at the strange thing with my finger.

Kenneth Linde looked in the direction and shrugged.

"That? It's a gliding jellyfish," he answered. "It's a type of flier... usually a collective organism. The accumulation of many creatures which decided that there is strength in numbers. The jellyfish are an exception, that is one creature that, as it were, absorbs its congeners, building organelles out of them. In general, it hunts anything that moves. Fortunately, it's high up, so we are not in danger."

"Flyers are usually not dangerous for us," Jamie butted in, who clearly didn't like staying on the sidelines for too long. "They hunt for small quarry. Only jellyfish can be dangerous, since they are poisonous and absorb the victim through the cup. Those appendages are their stinging tentacles. In some varieties, there are whole swirls of them, and when unfolded, they can reach several dozens of meters around them."

"What do they catch with them?" only now did I realize what was missing here. There were no birds. Not even one. One might expect that such a primitive world would be teeming with them, but no.

"Mostly young reptiles. They also won't pass up harpoids if they run across one. Although these are too agile, and the jellyfish are slow."

I suddenly remembered where I had already seen such a creature. In one of my father's huge holoalbums, I once observed images of extinct marine animals, including jellyfish. One of the species looked very similar. I remembered them because I thought they looked different. However, it's a different matter seeing a holographic image, and something of the like gliding overhead. Fortunately, it was already moving further away, majestically moving the edges of the cups. Jamie continued to chat, but I hardly listened to her. I felt very tired and I had a headache again.

Fortunately, we were almost at our destination. The car stopped at one of many nearly identical container houses at the foot of a high mountain. It was not visible from afar, but now I realized that all the slopes of the mountain are covered with unusual carvings: entrances, exits, stairs, even the shafts of external elevators. Window openings glittered in the sun with smooth glass. All this made a strong impression even on me, an ignorant girl who could only guess what knowledge and technique was required to create such a miracle of architecture.

This must have been Stone City. I learned about it in the information folder I read at the adaptation center. Where they examined us after we woke up, but also made sure that we get to know our new home a little. Despite all my admiration for these unusual buildings, I was secretly glad that we didn't go towards it, but to the Cynthia estate instead. As I understood, it was here that the administrative and technical core of the colony lived, in one-story houses built according to a single scheme from standard elements. On Earth, ones like these were built for the poorest in the working-class sections, but they also had other purposes – for example, when someone needed temporary housing. These here were most likely also supposed to be temporary, but it turned out differently. The residents clearly didn't want to move. Almost all of them have been expanded in the past, to resemble two or three typical living containers piled together.

The house of the doctor and his quiet wife outwardly didn't stand out as anything special. It was gray, squatted and, like most others, surrounded by a small garden. There was no corridor. From the garden, you entered through the front door directly into the 'living room', originally being one with the kitchenette. The kitchen was now separated from the rest of the room by a tall screen with a curtain instead of a traditional door.

The living room has been furnished with utmost care, trying to achieve at least the appearance of elegance. I could not deny the tenants their artistic taste, although the result looked more like old prints than a modern apartment. It was so rustic that I was almost surprised to see a holographic screen attached to the table.

"Sit down, my dear," the sharp-eared hostess of the house finally untied her tongue. Here she was the commander. She motioned me to a low, leather-upholstered sofa. "Would you like something to drink? We have fruit juice as well as coffee and tea from the local sources."

"I'd like some tea," I answered hesitantly. Local sources? I had little faith in what had grown up on an alien planet. But I decided that I would have to eat it anyway, so I need to break through as soon as possible.

Tina Roberts was bustling about, and after a while brought a full tray. On a low table she placed the mugs, a jug of steaming contents, a thin decanter of dark syrup, and a large plate of cookies. Jamie, who was sitting next to me, immediately started eating them. At first, I carefully tasted the tea – it tasted rather good, though it was very bitter.

"Pour in some syrup," Linde said and moved the decanter towards me. "Patrisian tea contains more tannins than what they give on earth so it requires more sweetening."

He sat in a large armchair opposite the sofa and looked at me anxiously. I thought I must be a real problem for him, and I felt terrible about it. I poured the syrup into the tea and drank it slowly in small sips. I didn't even touch the cookies.

"Dear Aura Maria," he finally began, "we know your unusual situation. The Solises told us everything before going on the expedition. They asked us to help acclimate you to Patris, to take care of you. You see, Patris is not a refuge for the socially unadapted. People who come here are tested and trained, and yet accidents still happen," he sighed. "You are not like that. No offense."

I nodded to show that I understood everything. Obviously, I could not be compared with the people selected in the respective centers, and I ended up on Patris as an intruder, not a colonist. I knew that well.

"Don't be like that, Ken," Tina interjected. "After all, this whole situation is not Aura Maria's fault. Whether she is adapted or not, she is here now, so let's focus on that."

Linde shrugged slightly.

"I'm not accusing her of anything, I'm just saying what the situation is. A colony is a place where everyone must be in some way useful to the whole, and what can you do?"

I opened my mouth and closed it. I didn't know what to say. They looked at me expectantly.

"I've been messing around a bit," I finally muttered, "I can repair things and put them together from parts."

"And what else?"

"I sing, paint and dance. I finished a virtual classical ballet course, level high..." I fell silent, knowing how ridiculous it sounded. I bowed my head over the cup. "Why did Aunt Estrella die?" I asked, wanting to change the topic of conversation at any cost.

The doctor cleared his throat.

"It's a long story," he said evasively. "Let's focus on you right now. The matter of your employment will have to be solved later. I'm sure we'll figure something out. For now, let's focus on what's the most urgent. We have already decided that you will live in Etta's hut. We would be too cramped for one more person."

"But I was supposed to take it when I grow up!" Jamie protested loudly.

He raised his hand to interrupt her lament.

"One more thing. Each new family, or a single person, receives a local guardian for the time of adaptation. Patris is not as safe as we would like it to be. In your case, the twins were supposed to be your guardians, but as you already know, they are currently on an expedition and will not return soon. We both have a responsible job that takes up most of our time. So I think Jamie should be your guide and roommate for now."

The girl didn't seem pleased, on the contrary, and I understood her well. She was at a difficult age, and the last thing she wanted was to look after an older cousin.

"I have to study," she moaned, "otherwise I won't pass the exams. I belong to the mentors and the chess team! And next week I was supposed to go to camp at the Eastern Mountains..."

Tina Roberts got up from her chair, as if she wanted to add weight to her words. I realized that even this stout, stern woman, the head of the local police, didn't know how to deal with the wayward teenager.

"Listen, Gemma, life is not just all fun and games! You keep whining that you're an adult and that we treat you like a child. Well, come to terms with the fact that growing up is primarily duties, not privileges."

"But mom Tina! It's not fair!" she turned towards me abruptly. "Aura Maria, please say something..."

Under her pleading gaze, I felt even more helpless. The whole situation was very awkward for me. I didn't know what I could say or whether my words would change anything. I was a stranger here; I knew neither these people nor the living situations. How could I get involved in anything?

The door creaked slightly and Raul entered the living room. As he moved, it was even more difficult to believe that he was not a real person, only the ruthless calm emanating from him broke this illusion.

"Doctor Meiller asks you to come to the hospital," he said to Kenneth. "Mrs. Abebi has contractions every five minutes."

Jamie's eyes lit up as she looked at him.

"Raul could live with you!" she exclaimed happily. "You don't have anything against robots, do you? He knows a lot, will even cook your dinner. And you'll be safe with him."

"I don't know..." I hesitated. I looked at her parents, who simply threw up their hands.

"That's a great solution," the girl got completely carried away with her idea. "Everyone will be satisfied. Take him, I'm telling you! Come on, I'm giving him to you."

"Don't make such decisions so rashly..." Linde began, but she cut him off with a wave of her tanned hand.

"Shut up, dad Ken, you have no say in this matter. Raul is mine, from my mother, and I can give him to anyone I want to. I don't need him, and he only annoys me. To tell you the truth, I hate him and I would have gotten rid of him long ago if you would have let me. All my colleagues laugh at me for having an electric nanny. Wait, I'll get his papers right away."

She ran away before I could say anything else. I looked at the android standing by the door, still like a statue. Dr. Linde sighed loudly.

"Forgive me, Aura Maria," he said, "maybe she's right, and that's for the best. I'm sorry, I need to go to the hospital. Rihanna Abebi has a narrow pelvis, so the birth is going to be difficult."

He left and then Jamie returned, triumphantly carrying a hardback technical passport in computer foil. I've seen them before. On the last page was the section: *Notes about owners*. She opened it on this page and entered with an electromagnetic stylus a new position: *Transfer of ownership*.

"You have to do this," she explained, brushing back a strand of auburn hair that had fallen over her eyes. "Otherwise, he will still consider me his mistress. And he should be taking care of you now and finally leave me the heck alone."

"I hope you don't regret this one day," Tina looked so unhappy that I decided to protest faintly. But it was useless. It seemed that Jamie will always get what she wants, no matter what anyone has to say about it. Clearly, she wasn't concerned with anyone or anything.

V

Aunt Estrella's cottage was smaller and slightly out of the way. It was locked up after the death of the tenant, waiting until Jamie becomes independent and decided to take over it. In the meantime, I had to start living here under the supervision of an android. I feel overwhelmed, unable to understand this planet or my own footing. I got the impression that I was dreaming about all of this. Regardless, I was thinking surprisingly clearly and could see that the Linde family was just trying to get rid of me. I was an unpleasant and unwanted guest for them. I didn't know why. They didn't know me. Maybe they were simply reluctant towards anyone interfering with their small, orderly world, although it still made me feel quite terrible.

I didn't feel like looking around the cabin, in my eyes small like a tool shed or a prison cell. Anyway, what was there to see? I didn't feel like unpacking either. I sat down helplessly in one of the chairs and began crying. All this was beyond me – to break out of a safe, loving home and throw myself into a completely unknown world, where no one cared about me and where I was something unwanted. I had no idea what to do here and how I would even find myself on this alien planet, when even my unseen cousins have returned home. Never before have I had to worry about anything related to my daily life. Father and uncle took care of everything. I didn't even know where the food in our kitchen or other necessities came from, and I never worked. How could I suddenly become a self-sufficient person? By what miracle?

I cried so much that I remembered about Raul only when he walked up next to me. I was stunned from surprise, and he hugged me and began stroking my head as if he was comforting a child.

"Everything will be fine," he said. Nothing more. The sound of his voice sounded so warm and soothing that I clung tightly against him, as I did with my father, and I sobbed loudly until I cried out all my tears. Only then did I calm down a little, completely exhausted. Raul got up, took me in his arms, carried me to the bed and covered me with a soft blanket. Then he sat down beside me and took my hand with his cool thin fingers.

"Sleep, Domina," he said. "It will calm you down and make you stronger. And tomorrow everything will seem less scary."

His words were so... human that tears again began to gather in my eyes.

"Stay with me until I fall asleep," I said. "Don't go anywhere."

"I won't go," he promised.

Calmed down, I closed my eyes.

He must have taken his promise very seriously because when I woke up he was still sitting by my bed, not even changing his position. I felt better, maybe not well, but I didn't feel like crying anymore, and I began to think clearly. Whether what happened was good or bad, I couldn't change it, so I had to adapt to the new situation. Crying wouldn't help me. There was no one here that it would work on.

I threw back the covers and sat up. I was still in my travel clothes. Yesterday I was shaking so much that I didn't even think to change into my nightgown, and besides, my things were still in my suitcases. The thought of unpacking them did not even occur to me yesterday, but today – rested and relaxed – I was ready to face the new situation.

"Shall I make you some tea, Domina?" Raul asked. "Or maybe some local coffee? They say that it's delicious."

"Do we even have coffee here?" I was surprised.

"Yes, Domina. Before your arrival, Mrs. Roberts tidied up the house and filled the pantry well."

I thought of the doctor's wife and my heart grew warm. Perhaps the woman with a stern face thought that I was a little in the way, but, nevertheless, she took care the house has some minimal comfort, which from now on will be mine. This was the first time I thought of it that way. Yes, it may be strange and small, but it's now mine. I looked around. I noticed what I hadn't seen yesterday: clean floors and walls, colored curtains on the clean windows. The blanket that covered me at night must have been washed recently. It smelled like soap and fruit oil, same as the pillow covers. This must be Tina Roberts' work. She didn't need to do this, and yet she thought about my well-being and took her time to improve it.

"Make that coffee," I said. Suddenly I was very curious about new tastes. Yesterday I got acquainted with tea, which was not bad, it reminded me of the Earth's red tea, semi-fermented. "Is there any sweetener for it?"

"Sugar syrup."

"That will do. And some toasts, if there are any. Do we have a toaster?"

"No. But Mrs. Roberts left some cookies for you. Should I bring them?"

"Yes, but not right now. First, I'm going to wash and change if I can find any clothes. I need to unpack."

My suitcases were still in the corner of the hall where I left them yesterday. Raul brought them into the bedroom and laid them on the bed so that I could freely browse the contents. Truth be told, until now I didn't even know what was in them. My father packed them, while I was lying in my room crying. And at the local rehab center, I used the clothes that were given to all new colonists during the tests and rest after hibernation. It was difficult for me to chase away the memories. I pressed my thumb against the lock of the smaller one. It flashed green, confirming the fingerprint code, and opened with a slight click. My eyes widened in surprise.

Inside was my dancer costume with a spare skirt and two pairs of professional pointe shoes. I remembered the problems that my father went through to get them for me. He had to order them custom made, for the last two hundred years they had not sewn adult sizes for this profession. After all, there was no human ballet anywhere on the globe. This function was taken over by holograms, and only children learned to dance as part of the stimulation of movements. And a small group of amateurs like me. I climbed deeper into the suitcase. Under a layer of thin plexiglass, I found several thick drawing blocks, a large box of pencils of different hardness, a pack of charcoal, a set of paints and brushes, and three cans of varnish. The rest of the space was taken by my favorite DIY tools and...

"Rudzia!" I shouted, pulling out a transparent box. My squirrel was inside it, curled up in a ball and motionless. I took it out and looked around anxiously. How did she survive the trip? Did she even survive? Turned off for such a long time, her fragile processors could be damaged. I didn't even know if the cargo holds of the ship, I was on was properly protected, and in the end, solar flares can damage any electronics.

The emergency button didn't work. I took out a bag with a suitable set of tools from my suitcase, took Rudzia into the living room and laid it on the table. I felt the magnetic clips in the fluffy fur, let go of them and opened the hatch, behind which the activation mechanism was hidden. As I suspected, the sensors were completely covered in residue. I carefully cleaned the interior, fixed any connections that seemed in danger, and closed the lid. I pressed the switch again.

This time, Rudzia immediately twitched and blinked her black eyes. She wiggled her nose, licked her face, and stretched slowly, twitching her ears. Then she clucked, ruffled her tail and climbed onto my shoulder.

"An android animal... unusual," said Raul, who stood behind me all the time and watched what I was doing. I could swear that I heard admiration in his voice.

"In a way," I said. "When I was still very young, my dad bought me her as a pet. I had no friends, so I became attached to her, maybe more than I should have. Dad knew that, so he put her in my suitcase," I couldn't help but shed a few tears. "He packed her with me so that I would not feel lonely. Plus, my dance costume, tools and pencils... Everything I loved, everything except himself. He couldn't pack that for me. I am so scared that I will never see him again..."

Rudzia yelped sympathetically, gently rubbed her lips against my cheek and wrapped her tail around my neck. Like all toys of this type, it had a built-in emotion reader. So she responded flawlessly to certain behaviors and, thanks to the feedback, only listened to me and played only with me. She ignored other people and left even when they wanted to pet her. I had no idea how many independent actions there were. It had to be something, since such artificial pets were equipped with the same processors as in androids, only in minimal quantities. But the program was responsible for most of the reflexes. Apparently, it's an obvious fact, but as a child I was greatly delusioned that my pet simply loved me.

Suddenly Raul took my hand. He didn't say anything, just held my hand and I found his touch calming and inspiring, so much so that I even managed to smile.

"Enough of these lamentations," I carefully wiped my nose. "I have to start getting accustomed here. After all, this is my new home."

I have never done heavy housework before, only some light ones. It wasn't necessary since there was mechanical service at my family home that took care of everything, even folded clothes that I threw on a chair before going to bed. But not here. I didn't know yet if only my home was so primitive or if all of them were, but something told me that it wasn't going to be anything like back on Earth here, and I needed to get used to it. No amount of crying could help me, and there was no longer my father in whose arms I could hide from the whole world. I guess I could say that I was forced to grow up quickly – from the child that I've been until now, I would have to become an independent woman in a world that I did not know.

I was settling in the entire afternoon, hanging my modest supply of clothes in the closet and arranging the equipment so that the interior of the house seemed a little cozier. It was not easy, but in the end, with the help of Raul, I achieved a rather satisfactory result. While doing so, I also found something I didn't know about – a module for connecting to the colony's radio center. I had no idea that such an archaic solution existed here, but on reflection, I thought it made sense. I had to tinker a bit with the device, but I was able to get it to work. Live music poured out of the speaker and it immediately became more cheerful. The broadcast was interrupted by small announcements and some local news. So far, I couldn't understand a lot, I didn't know the local realities yet, but for some unknown reason I felt better. The loud voices of the announcers and the DJ lifted the mood and chased away the feeling of loneliness. They made me realize that I am among people, in a close community. I wasn't part of it yet, but I was starting to hope that I could be.

At about two o'clock in the afternoon, someone rang the doorbell. Raul opened it and Jamie ran in with a large, covered dish in her hands.

"Hey!" she called. "Mom Tina is sending you some dinner! In fact, there are two servings here, so I'll eat with you here, not at home. And by the way, I can answer any questions you have, since I'm sure you have a lot of them. Do you mind?"

"No, not at all," I was even glad to see her. I really started to like her, and I wanted her to like me too. But would that even be possible?

Raul brought plates and cutlery.

"Jamie, what do you know about me?" I asked cautiously, when the girl deliberately divided the food on the plate – pieces of roast, some green vegetables and something resembling French fries, but probably not from potatoes.

She sat down opposite me and began to eat greedily. I've tried it too. The dish turned out to be very tasty, although unlike anything I've tried before. The meat was definitely not a substitute because it contained small cubes and cartilage, and the fries tasted more like fried cauliflower.

"Well, I know you're my mom's niece. And that you had to flee Earth because you were in trouble with the law."

"Well, maybe not exactly," I sighed. "You know, Jamie... I have... low IQ."

"What do you mean, how?" she looked at me in surprise. She had beautiful, long, deep blue eyes, probably after her father, because they didn't remind me of any other family member. Such a shade of deep blue, almost makes me want to say that so bright that I've never seen such in anyone's life.

"Just like that. My tests were always bad, and after a childhood illness it got even worse. I couldn't even master the regular school curriculum. Dad managed to keep me from being deported to a labor colony, but the social commission finally found out about it. But they decided that I was too old to adapt. They wanted to put me into euthanasia."

My cousin didn't seem to care too much.

"Our laws are less strict," she said with a full mouth. "I know that social engineering is sometimes overdone on Earth. I'm glad I don't live there."

"Why?" I popped another piece of meat into my mouth. It was really delicious. "You probably wouldn't have any problems there. You are smart."

She smiled broadly.

"IQ is not the only thing that's important, Aura Maria. Here it's very clear. On this planet. I know the theory of generational planning, we were taught that in history lessons... these methods eliminate many problems, but create others. In fact, I don't think would be put into euthanasia, although your father might have thought they were going to do so."

"How can you be so sure?"

She put down her fork and made a serious expression that did not match her half-childish face.

"A few years ago, a professor of applied social engineering, Akira Hanako, joined us. He was at school giving a lecture. Among other things, he said that there is a special, semi-secret unit that uses the talents of burdened people in the social field... those with low IQs, but who also have, for example, exceptional manual skills. Apparently, the liquidation of such units was completely abandoned. But I'm glad you came here anyway," she added with a wide smile.

Hmmm... I wasn't convinced. Perhaps this professor was telling the children the truth, or maybe exactly what they wanted to hear. Since the people living in the colony changed their views on how childbirth should look like and what is important in life, the rules on Earth may seem cruel or even absurd to them. And if so...

"How did it happen that the colonists changed their ways of thinking?" I asked

Jamie swallowed what was in her mouth and eagerly began explaining.

"They discovered a settlement here, founded by the participants of the previous expedition, which was considered lost. They didn't follow the rules of genetic selection because they saw no reason to. They were sure that they would die soon anyway. Then, when it turned out that this wouldn't come so quickly, it was a little late. After an initial panic, they realized that children with unclean genetics were children like any other, and that even if they were considered inferior, they were doing well. When the team of Captain Willner, my father, arrived, they were at first surprised and shocked, but then... you know, aunt, people started thinking that maybe we Earth's rules are not entirely just. In any case, you can forget about them in new conditions. When they realized that fertility was an issue here, every child became valuable, and in the end, everyone was saved at any cost."

It sounded very interesting and overall, I liked this idea. For a long time, I've been thinking about why one newborn is given a chance, and another one is not. Due to the fact that I did not go to school, I didn't have the opportunity to receive overall indoctrination, so some things were not as obvious to me as they were to my peers. I ate and thought about it all, looking at my young cousin. I saw in her more and more the resemblance to my father. At first it wasn't so obvious, but after spending some time with her, talking to her, it became more obvious. She had not only similar facial features, but also the same way of looking, the same smile, even the shape of her neck, even the expression on her face. That's probably why I felt sympathetic to this kid from the start, although I clearly saw that she was selfish, wayward and does not respect any authorities. However, I had to honestly admit that at the same time she was so full of life and joy so much so that you could involuntarily feel happier when in her company.

"Tell me, Jamie, what should I do in this month of freedom that Tina talked about?" I asked.

"Anything you want," she said cheerfully. "Just get to know the colony, explore the surroundings, go to Stone City, meet people. Just take Raul with you wherever you go, he knows all about what is dangerous here and what to avoid. And he knows the area, he will not get lost."

I looked at Raul. He stood by the window with his usual, unintelligible expression on his face.

„Why were you so eager to get rid of him?"

Jamie also looked at the android, smiled and waved her hand at him in a friendly manner.

"I just wanted him to finally start stalking someone other than me," she explained. "He's incredibly intrusive. It didn't bother Mom, but it bothers me terribly. If not for that, I could even like him."

The mention of Estrella Solis turned my mind in a different direction.

"Why did your mother die?" I asked "Was it an accident?"

"No. It's a complicated matter. You see, there is a species of frogs that lives here, of which secretions are capable of repairing any damage to the body, based on the DNA code. It even leads to the absorption or removal of artificial implants and their replacement with original organs. Therefore, despite the blockage of the fallopian tubes, my mother was able to get pregnant and give birth to me. At first, everyone thought that we had an elixir of immortality, but then it turned out that this same factor over time causes some changes in the blood of mammals, and this causes mini-blood clots and, finally, extensive brain damage. The capillaries can't handle it, you know. They even discovered it quite quickly, but no antidote could be found. Several people from the Viking expedition died in this way, including my mother."

"It's a shame," I whispered. I was very sorry that I wouldn't get the chance to meet my father's sister. "But what did you mean when you said that there are fertility problems here?"

Jamie finished her portion and pushed the plate away, resting her elbows on the table.

"Because there just are, nobody knows why exactly. The first group of colonists brought their children with them, but then few could boast of a full-term pregnancy. Hah, even one that began at all! Those from the minus one expedition were more fortunate," she became lost in thought for a moment. "Although maybe not entirely. In fact, they did not have many children. If not for the Vikings and the supply of fresh blood, they would have died out as a result of inbreeding."

I hardly understood any of this.

"Of what expedition?" my head began to spin.

"From the first research trip to Patris. A large group of scientists from different fields, about a hundred odd crew members," the girl explained patiently. "They started a settlement here when they lost contact with the Earth and realized that they could not launch their ship and fly away. Dr. O'Reilly told us in class that they succumbed to depression and were only saved by working on the basics. The Viking expedition found them only a few decades later, when the firstborn on Patris had long since had children. They don't have such problems. O'Reilly says this is because we are still introduced species, while they are already local."

She mentioned that name again. This man was probably something of a local authority.

"Who is Dr. O'Reilly?" I asked.

"That's our main magician of all kinds of electronics. Especially robots. He is often called the *doctor of androids*. He's a funny old man, lives not far from here. He was friends with my mom."

I finished dinner and only then asked my next question.

"So, there are other androids here besides Raul?"

"Oh yes, a few dozen. Of both sexes, so to speak," she laughed. "Doesn't that sound funny? The sex of a robot?"

"I'm still here," Raul said suddenly, making me jump up on the chair.

"I know," Jamie didn't seem embarrassed. "Don't worry, Aura Maria, that's how he is, sometimes when he says something, he almost seems human."

I looked at Raul and I would swear that I saw a trace of some kind of emotion on his smooth face – offense? Dislike? Pain? *Impossible,* I thought. He thought for himself, there was no doubt about that, but emotions are a completely different matter. You can't program them, even I knew that, and I know nothing about AI.

There was a sound resembling a trumpet outside the window.

"Sal is here to pick me up!" Jamie was delighted, immediately forgetting what we were talking about.

I looked out the window. Through the courtain I saw one of the local cars and a dark-haired boy at the wheel. Jamie jumped up from the table, nearly dropping her plate to the floor.

"I'll be leaving now, aunt! We have a fundraiser today before leaving for summer camp. Do you remember what I said? Don't be angry that I didn't want to live with you and be your guide, but that trip is so important to me, you wouldn't even know..."

The horn sounded outside the window again. The girl turned around on her heels, and then disappeared from my sight. I felt a sting of jealousy. She was so free, so full of life and joy, that she made me painfully aware of my own shortcomings. After all, I grew up sheltered, almost completely isolated from the outside world. I didn't gossip with my friends because I didn't have any. I didn't date boys because I didn't even have a chance to, hah! I didn't even know a single one. Because how would I? When? For the first time, I thought that, wanting the best, my father accidentally hurt me.

I didn't feel like walking around a completely new area. I wasn't ready yet. But I needed to somehow begin getting to know it.

"Raul, is there some kind of... city network?" I asked.

"Yes, Domina," he answered hastily. "Should I turn on the computer."

I looked around in surprise.

"Where is it?"

The android first collected the dishes from the table, and then pressed the previously invisible button under the table top. The boards parted to reveal a keyboard, and behind it rolled out a large screen – not a holographic one, but made of a translucent sheet. Technology from a century ago is probably easier to come by on this planet.

I touched the tiny, raised keys. The screen lit up, revealing the starting screen. The operation of it identical to the devices I knew, so I quickly found what I needed. This was something that fit me – distance learning. Before I went on my first solo walk, I needed to know as much as possible about this planet, this colony and these people.

VI

Two days passed before I finally dared to leave the house. During this time, I remotely learned the structure of the colony and all its surroundings. Among other things, I learned that the Stone City, intricately carved into the slopes of a high mountain, is the administrative center. The colonists' apartments were located on the edges, so that people had windows they could look out to the outside. On the other hand, offices and utility rooms such as bathrooms, playrooms and rentals were located deeper. Many families preferred to live in the City rather than in a residential area at the foot of the mountain, as it was more convenient and safer. I understood these people well. The nature surrounding the estate was undeniably beautiful, although it differed from everything known on Earth and therefore was a little frightening. It could also be dangerous, especially to children, who are by nature reckless. The city practically guaranteed 100% safety, and its many amenities made life easier and more enjoyable.

I had the sincere intention to explore all the secrets of both the planet and the colony before going out on my first walk, but just two days later I got the feeling that I was suffocating in this cramped house. I was also lonely. I was supposedly used to it, but not quite – even when my father and uncle were not at home, I knew they would be back. Now I had only Raul, and he was not enough for me. From what Jamie said, Aunt Estrella treated him like an equal, but I couldn't. I won't say I didn't like him, but he could not drown out my loneliness and longing for another person. Once again, in the evenings, I talked to Silver – I was afraid that he would not be here while I was on Patris, but he was. If I had to explain to someone how... I wouldn't be able to. On one hand, I knew that Silver was a product of my mind, but on the other hand, for me he was a completely real person, endowed with a kind of autonomy. And I was able to speak to him with complete honesty.

Raul didn't pay attention to it. The first time he entered the 'bedroom' (which is funny, as it was about the size of a large closet), attracted by my voice, he seemed confused. He looked around slightly, then looked at me, slightly tilting his head towards his left shoulder. He saw me talking, but he could not figure out with whom, and this caused him 'cognitive problems. I knew this term from the Internet, and it fit like a glove.

"I'm talking to my imaginary brother," I explained to him. "Don't worry, I'm not crazy. I was very lonely since childhood and needed company."

He took note of this without comment. He was generally restrained; he spoke only when I asked him about something or when the situation required it. Little by little, I began to understand Jamie's reluctance to be with his company, but at the same time, I tried my best to accept him as he is. I knew that he was my ally no matter what and something of a guardian whom I could trust. And this was important because I was completely unfamiliar with this environment and could easily create trouble for myself.

Having decided to go and see the area, I first of all informed Raul about my intention. I needed a guide and guardian. After all, for my whole life, I did not go farther than the garden by myself, and I would not dare to walk away from my current apartment alone. That's right, walk... I wasn't much of a walker. Nowadays, hiking was not very popular at all, and I also did not have the opportunity to do it, since my overly protective father hid me in the shadows. I wouldn't go far.

"Not a problem," Raul assured me and brought a strange car out from under a covered shelter next to the house. It resembled a low, narrow platform on four wheels of a strange design.

"What is that?"

"Electroboard," he explained. "Short for *electronic board*. It has control knobs at the front, which also serve to keep the driver upright. The rudder column contains all the electronics. Runs on a battery, just like bigger vehicles. It's charged by a solar panel on the roof of the carport. It's not suitable for long trips, but it will do for driving around the area."

I listened to him with one ear, squatting and concentrating on the wheels of the device. They looked as if each of them consisted of two separates, which, in turn, consisted of many independently rotating rollers. I immediately figured out that this design allows the small, primitive-looking vehicle to move in any direction and in almost any terrain. I remembered something similar from popular science programs. It was called *Ezekiel's Wheel* and although I could not understand where the name came from, I liked it. Design details like these always interested me more than anything.

"Let's go, then," I said, getting up. "I'm very curious to see how you drive such a thing."

"For now, I'll drive, Domina. It takes a little practice. Please hug me tightly around the waist."

I stood behind him on the platform and put my arms around his waist as instructed. At first, I hid behind the android's back as best I could so that no one noticed me. I only mustered up the courage when I realized that they were not paying attention to me, busy with their own affairs. I was able to concentrate on observing the area. And it was beautiful, like the pictures in the books about the Earth's past. The estate stretched out to the very foot of Stone City, and there were many flowers between the houses. It was hard to believe that this was not video art, but living vegetation around me. It looked a little different than on Earth – it was bigger and the colors were more saturated, really strong and deep, like in surreal paintings. They grew at the edges of streets, in gardens and outside the estate, where they turned into a huge forest. Some trees also grew near the houses, casting shadows on them. It looked as if the inhabitants of the colony couldn't live without them. It was as if they were reacting to the fact that they had so little to do with it back on Earth.

What surprised me the most was that the trees on Patris had a different structure than on Earth. I looked at a few of them and realized where this sense of difference came from. The main trunk was replaced by flexible shoots intertwined in a twisted bunch, from which the branches of the crown grew, often much thicker than the individual component of the 'trunk'. I had the impression that something was alive inside each such bundle, but so far, I have not had the courage to check it. I have always had an irrational fear of insects and small creatures like lizards and mice. I was very ashamed of this, but I could not control it."

"Can these plants be touched?" I asked Raul.

On Earth there were strict rules – wild trees, flowers and even grass planted by the city council were not allowed to be touched with your hands, not to mention that no one without ECO certification was allowed to even enter the areas where they grew. Although the same rules applied even in parks where video art was combined with natural flowers. Of course, it was possible to take care of some species at home, but that wasn't the same.

"Nobody forbids it, Domina," he replied, "but not all of them are safe for humans. If you are not properly dressed, it's best to avoid venturing into the forest."

"I didn't want to go there at all," I shuddered at the thought. "It must be full of bugs."

"If you mean small arthropods, there are almost none of them here. Certainly not in the immediate vicinity of the estate. Patris has very little insects, and most of them hide from the human eye."

"And what about the other animals?"

"Reptiles and amphibians. Many types. The smallest are seven millimeters long and play the same role in the ecosystem as insects on Earth," he said mechanically, like an automatic reader. "The astrobiology department takes care of cataloging them. To date, five thousand seven hundred and eighteen species of reptiles and four thousand and sixteen species of amphibians have been catalogued..."

I looked at the darkening wall of the forest in front of me, of which shades of green were in places intertwined with the colors of flowers, large and fleshy. I didn't want to go there at all, especially when I thought about the seven-millimeter amphibians that lived there. I was glad that they at least weren't at the estate. I would probably lose my mind if they started crawling on my bed.

"Maybe I'll go there someday, but not now," I decided. "For now, I want to focus on the human settlements."

"There are a lot of them," Raul waved his other hand, still holding the wheel.

"Show me. And tell me about everything."

He perked up noticeably and added gas. I looked around, listening to what he was saying and soaking up an interesting view of the different areas of the estate. Each of them was slightly different from the other, mainly in the dominant color of the fences and facades of the houses. This probably played a significant role. Houses closer to Stone City, just like mine, seemed older and were mostly dark green or steel in color, natural for composite containers. Those further away, although modular, were already painted and even stenciled.

Finally, Raul made a wide arc with the electric board, and then directed it into the mountainous area near the estate. We drove up to a profiled slope and stopped. The hill, as I found out right now, was a sort of viewing platform from which you could see the whole area. It had comfy benches, tables, and even beach umbrellas, and must have been used for picnics during vacations. Now it was empty, and I could freely look around, examining the estate and the surrounding forest from above. I could clearly see the river, the nearby lake, and then the mountain range. And somewhere very far, on the horizon, I could even see the seashore. There was also a good view of Stone City from here. Glittering windows of apartments in granite walls were clearly visible from a height, giving the impression that the entire mountain is covered with mica tiles.

I walked around the terrace observing the visible areas. From one side, there was an automated farm area stretching almost to the horizon, while a large industrial and production complex hid the Stone City. From time to time, a cloud of water vapor would appear over one of the filter domes covering the factory chimneys and slowly dissolve in the air. The smoke cleaning system worked flawlessly. I vaguely remembered the parameters of an industrial particle filter – 1/500000, which meant that there could be only one particle of any pollutant for five hundred thousand molecules of pure water. I didn't know whether that was a lot or a little, my ability to judge such proportions was never good. But judging by the way the clouds of water evaporated, it should have been clean. Every possible effort has been made to ensure that the new home is not polluted.

I couldn't see any more human settlements. I don't think there were any, maybe separate research stations hidden among the forest hills. The colony concentrated around Stone City and expanded on the sides, slowly building up the free space with new houses. Based on what Roul had told me, not only did everyone not want to live at the Celine Estate, but the appartements carved out in granite were even much more desirable as they were more modern and comfortable. They were almost fought for.

"Why *Celine Estate*?" I asked.

"In honor of the fallen Dr. Xiao," he replied, moving smoothly from one topic to another without the slightest hesitation. "Her actions saved the Viking expedition. Her memory was honored in this way."

On the left, behind the industrial complex, I suddenly noticed a herd of some kind of animals leisurely strolling across the plain. They seemed very large and very calm.

"What's that?"

"Brenes. They always move in family groups. They are gentle and useful, because they eat up waste. You don't need to be afraid of them."

"Is there something I do need to be afraid of?" I looked inquiringly at the android.

"Yes. Some of the local fauna can be dangerous, such as predators or some fliers. However, they mostly avoid people. They inhabit the hills and plains. In forests, you need to be more careful about the small but poisonous creatures rather than large and predatory ones."

I looked at the forest again. It seemed endless.

"Does anyone live outside the estate and the city?"

"Not anymore, Domina."

"You mean that they did before?" it surprised me a little. Could there have been two estates?

"Yes, Domina. The village of the First lay in the forest."

Now I was completely dumbfounded. I looked at Raul questioningly, in silence, until I remembered the words of an engineer from the *Science Investigation* program that I had once watched with passion.

If, right after saying that you want to draw something, you tell an android: "I don't have a pencil", it will treat it as information and not as a disguised request for the object in question, which would be obvious to humans. We need to clearly articulate our expectations for artificial intelligence and convey them in a way that doesn't have any metaphors or understatements. Never assume that the android will understand what we mean.

This engineer, I think his last name was Karpinsky, called this reaction *technological autism* and claimed that it was due to the inability for the android brain to create a *general theory of the mind* – whatever that means. His words were very interesting, although he spoke in a terribly archaic tongue. It's not surprising, as the recordings presented in the program were probably a century old.

"Who are the First?" I finally asked.

"Descendants of Patris' manned research expedition. Their ship broke down, so they set up a makeshift colony there. They lived quite primitively, but survived. They even reproduced. At first, they did not want to integrate with the *newblood,* they were very distrustful of them, but after a while they decided that it was better to unite forces and build the future on this planet together."

Yes, the future... At the moment I could not imagine any of my own. What was I supposed to do here? I looked up at the cloudless sky, shimmering in different shades of blue, greenish and pink. Hanging low over the horizon, the sun with its own name *Jewel* also shimmered in different colors, like a masterly polished diamond. It was nearly unreal. At times, this fabulous space was crossed by shadows – creatures flying in the V formation, similar to birds, individual specimen or symbiotic colonies that take on a variety of forms, from simple rhombuses to the already familiar to me bowl-shaped, wavy at the edges with elongated so-called tentacles.

"It's so beautiful here," I whispered. "It's like a fairy tale, and yet I am afraid of this place. Do you know what fear is?"

Raul shook his head slowly.

"Not from my own experience, but I know that it is natural for human beings. It is a biological reflex that contributes to human survival."

Suddenly he took my hand, like when I cried on the first day.

I looked into his eyes, or rather what was their imitation. If I didn't know the truth, I would not have guessed – the eyes of the android looked completely human, they even gave the impression that they were slightly moist. But they couldn't express emotions, or at least they shouldn't. Nevertheless... It was only now that I noticed how long his eyelashes were. Aunt Estrella chose a really handsome android. I briefly wondered if it was a factory design or if she had specially ordered him somehow.

"Thank you," I muttered and immediately after added: "Will you teach me how to drive the electric board?"

"Oh, it's very simple," he let go of my hand. "Any child here knows how to do it. Look: here, where you put your feet, there are two protrusions at the level of the toes. The right one is for acceleration, the left one is for hard braking if necessary. You have a handbrake on the left stick and a gear selector on the right. You choose your direction by turning the steering column. The center display shows speed in miles per hour and battery charge status. Simple. Want to give it a try?"

"With pleasure!"

By the time we got home, I already knew how to drive this simple vehicle. Raul stood behind me and helped me imperceptibly, lightly touching my hands if necessary. I thought that he would have been an excellent teacher – why weren't androids used in such roles? There was probably a reason. Maybe they weren't completely trusted? I wished I had someone to talk to about this. Dr. Linde and his wife were still at work and I was too embarrassed to ask them for help. They had their own lives and I was practically nothing to them. Not even a relative. Just a girl, whom they hardly know, brought to their attention by their neighbors. And the cousin of their pupil. I could wonder for a long time what that means to them emotionally, but I suspected that it meant nothing. Jamie... it's clear she was mainly thinking about herself. Aunt Estrella's android remained the only creature that somewhat cared about me. And the only one alone just like me.

VII

On that day, Raul was not with me. In the morning, Dr. Linde called me and with embarrassment asked me to lend him my android for a dozen hours or so. He needed help at the hospital. One of the research ships returned from the depths of the land in a terrible state, the crew needed urgent help. He didn't give me any details, but I realized that the researchers must have been in serious trouble. Raul had a medical degree and once helped regularly at the hospital. As I learned, Aunt Estrella wanted him to live the way he wanted, but after her death it was considered a harmless quirk, since, after all, there were no legal rules for treating an android the same as a person. By the decision of the colony council, Raul became Jamie's property... her adoptive parents also thought it was for the best, but Dr. Linde occasionally sought for his help at the hospital. For example, in situations like this.

Without Raul, my tiny house seemed empty and quiet. I tried to continue studying Patris from the computer, but nothing came of it. I felt lonely. Finally, I put Rudzia in my pocket and went for a walk. I already knew the surrounding area well, I explored it every evening, mostly on the electric board. Now I decided to leave it at home. I didn't feel like exploring this time, I just wanted to take a walk and get some fresh air. I had to think about what to do next. The day was approaching when I had to go to the local employment office and I still didn't know how to play that out. What will I tell to the coordinators? I had absolutely nothing to brag about.

It's funny, but riding the electric board under Raul's supervision, I visited the farthest corners of the colony, but didn't know the immediate surroundings very well. My neighbors were members of the *Vikings Expedition,* the founders of the colony, people who were at least twice my age. They had good manners, which meant that they did not interfere with the life of their new neighbor. They didn't have children because they couldn't have them — and that's a good thing, too. Of the young people in the area there was only Jamie, and she was still at summer camp. I could walk without fear of meeting children that would stare at me. As soon as I thought about them, I remembered that nasty girl from the ship. Yuck. I couldn't imagine being a mother and enduring such a thing every day. What a nightmare.

As I already found out, it was considered good manners here to not disturb strangers. At first, I thought that people knew something about me and therefore ignored me, but Raul corrected me.

"Patris has a different system of courtesy. First friendships are made at work, and the invasion of neighbors is something most inappropriate. If you want to visit someone or ask them to visit you, you leave a message in their mailbox outside the house."

I had no intention of doing so. Not yet, anyway. And I really liked that system, as it made me feel much safer. I could go anywhere and observe everything without being exposed to anyone's curiosity or obsession.

For these reasons, I was surprised by the voice clearly directed towards me.

"Hey, kid."

I looked around in confusion. I didn't even notice how immersed in my own thoughts I was, I approached the very edge of the district, from where there was an unobstructed view of Stone City.

The voice was coming from an older man sitting comfortably in a low chair outside the house. I paused, not knowing what to do.

"Hey kid," the old man repeated. "Without your guardian today?"

He smiled at me. And yet his angular face struck me as strangely sad, like the whole figure, thin and bony, like a man dying of hunger or seriously ill. He had pale blue faded eyes, very gray hair, and a shadow of stubble on his cheeks and chin.

"Good morning, sir," I muttered hesitantly. "Raul is at the hospital, helping Dr. Linda today."

The man became more serious.

"Oh yes, that accident. There are indeed many wounded. That's Linde for you... treats androids like vacuum cleaners, but when needed, he cannot live without them."

I looked at him with little understanding.

"Do you know me?"

He took a sip from the tall glass in his hand.

"In a way. I've been watching you since you moved here. I know that you arrived in the last transport and that you are a relative of the twins," he was silent for a moment. "They told me about you. Though they didn't mention that you were so pretty."

"What are you saying?" I was embarrassed.

"The truth. You don't have to take it as flirting. I'm too old for that and too married."

Instinctively, I looked for his wife. I didn't know if she would like my presence and fought the urge to get out of sight of the residents of this house.

"Astrid is on duty," my interlocutor immediately understood who I was looking for. "She was recently promoted to lieutenant, and it's becoming more and more rare for her to be at home. Plus, I'm sure you'd like her right away. She is such a sweet and kind person; you have no need to be afraid of her."

"I'm not afraid," I swallowed, trying to speak naturally.

"It's easy to see when I've been watching you. You've been here for almost a month now and you haven't gotten close to anyone, not even Linda and Roberts. You live alone in Etta Solis' former home, and her android takes care of you."

Under his gaze, I felt like a schoolgirl at the blackboard.

"Yes, Jamie gave him to me," I confirmed.

He became gloomier upon hearing that name.

"Jamie Willner... strange kid. She is like neither her mother nor her father. She's part of the local anthropocentric organization founded here by one of the younger folks. This means that she hates artificial intelligence and, to top it off, considers herself to be the smartest of the entire colony. I suppose she may have some right," he added after a moment. "Has a razor-sharp mind. Her personality is a little worse, though, because she rarely thinks about anything other than herself. What are you standing there for? Sit down."

He pointed to a garden bench. I sat down on the very edge, still terrified. He must have seen it because he smiled again.

"No need to be afraid of me, child. Don't make such a frightened face. I'm harmless. What is your name, actually? Would you like something to drink?"

"Aura Maria Solis, sir. And no, I don't feel thirsty, but thank you."

"Call me Mac. I'm MacLean O'Leary."

"Doctor of androids?" I blurted out. He raised his eyebrows slightly.

"You already know?"

"Jamie mentioned you, sir."

"That's nice of her. I hope you take better care of Raul than she did."

"Take care, which means...?"

"He needs teaching, attention... just like a person. Do you understand?"

There was a tone in the doctor's voice that clearly indicated great personal commitment. Suddenly, I felt a surge of empathy and trust. This *funny old man*, as Etta's daughter described him mockingly, really must have been somebody."

"Yes. Now I do," I replied and added as an excuse: "No one ever told me how to treat androids. I really don't know anything about them. I've only seen a few shows about AI."

"I'm always here if you need advice. You can always count on me and my better half. She was friends with Etta no less than me."

Now I smiled. I had to. I felt a strange warmth and, oddly enough, a sense of security, which I so lacked here.

"Oh, that's better. You have a sweet smile too. Once you start working, your fellow coworkers will lose their heads over you."

I felt a smile grow on my face. He noticed it immediately and raised his eyebrows slightly.

"So, I suppose you already know in which section you'd like to work?"

"I don't know," I admitted helplessly. "I have no idea. I can't do anything useful."

"Like this?"

"Well, you see, sir... Mac... I'm stupid," I blurted out in desperation.

This clearly intrigued him. He looked at me closely, like at an insect under a microscope.

"No, I don't think you are," he finally decided.

"Why don't you think so?"

He seemed surprised.

"Honey, I've met plenty of fools. Each of them was ready at any moment to blame the whole world for their stupidity, but never themselves. To say something like that, you'd have to be rather wise, I'd say."

It was nice of him to say that, but I was not convinced.

"But it is the truth."

"Why do you think so? Did you do poorly at school?"

"Yes. I mean, no... in fact, I didn't even go to a regular school. That is... I did at first, but then..."

I don't even know myself how it happened, but I suddenly began telling this person I barely knew the story of my life. Confessions literally poured out of me, flowed like an uncontrollable river. Maybe it was because he just listened, not stopping and not taking his penetrating gaze from me, encouraging me with a slight nod of his head whenever I sell silent for a moment. He seemed to be genuinely interested in what I wanted to say, although it didn't make any sense. Why would he care?

"Well, okay," he said when I finished. "So you didn't do well. But where did your inner conviction of your own stupidity come from?"

"What do you mean? The IQ tests... and the exam results... the teachers just threw up their hands. They said that they could not explain why I didn't learn knowledge like other children."

He waved his hand condescendingly.

"Intelligence tests are overrated. The gods were taken from humanity, they had to be replaced by something else, so that's where the cult of IQ came from. The fact is that intelligence comes in many different shades and is not always associated with the ability to solve mathematical puzzles. And that's what the official tests are based on."

This point of view surprised me, and I thought about it for a while. I found myself seeking arguments against his thesis, as if I were my own accuser.

"And the exams?" I finally asked. "I've failed almost all of them."

"That indicates social dysfunction, not stupidity. I don't know what happened to child psychology, when they can't recognize such a simple disorder. Instead of eliminating you, they should have given you therapy."

What he said made sense. I didn't want him to know what I was silent about – that my father was categorically against putting this issue in the hands of child psychologists. He claimed that they would try to make me mentally ill and put me in some institution. I think he really believed it.

"Well, is there nothing you can do?" O'Leary continued.

"There is something," I said hastily, "but nothing useful."

"What would that be?"

"I studied in the virtual. Classical dance, for example. I have completed the basic course, the advanced course, and almost the entire expert level."

Now I have managed to impress him. He whistled delightedly

"You've unlocked the expert level? I have not heard of anyone ever able to do so. Virtual instructors are very strict. And they cannot be bribed or convinced with tears. Show me what you can do. Come on, at least a little bit."

I got off the bench, took the *arabesque no. II* position and did the basic *pas*, *ballance* and a simple pirouette. There was little I could do in such uneven terrain, but the doctor seemed impressed."

"Bravo, amazing!" he exclaimed, clapping his hands. "I can imagine what you could do on a stage in a classical outfit"

I stopped halfway to the next move.

"Yes, but my father said it wouldn't do me any good. The same as singing. I learned that as well."

„Not in a professional sense," he agreed nonchalantly. "It's just a hobby these days. Holograms are the ones dancing in ballet. Their proliferation destroyed a certain artistic world... why torture girls and boys for years when you can program holograms? They don't get tired, they don't make mistakes, they don't need to exercise, they don't fight over money, and they don't become crippled by the age of thirty."

"Do you think it's better this way?" I asked with unexpected bitterness.

He threw up his hands.

"It depends on how you look at it. After ballet it was movies, it was the end of spoiled celebrities getting paid millions, and the entire industry benefited from it, although, on the other hand, all its glitter was lost. The whole mess associated with the profession ended, all its dirty deeds and abuses, all the absurdity of *being a star* was finally damned to hell. And then the same thing happened to the music industry... although I guess it finished itself off when computer processing of the recordings began. Talent ceased to matter, and when musicians died out from the era before, new ones stopped rising to their level. The holography of this sector was just a dot above the i. Why hire an unreliable person with his own requirements, if you can generate an artificial singer with the desired timbre, tone and octave range? The only status retained the authors of the texts, but nobody ever paid attention to them."

After these words, we both fell silent. After a moment, O'Leary sighed and resumed his investigation.

"So, you studied with hobby programs?"

"It wasn't the only thing," I began to speak and stopped, because at that moment Rudzia got tired of sitting in my pocket. She stuck her mouth out, clucked, then climbed onto my shoulder and began to wash her face with her front paws.

"What is that creature?" the doctor asked cheerfully.

"Ah, it's just an interactive squirrel from my childhood. I got it when I was eight."

"And it still works? That's amazing, these toys tend to break down quickly and are never repaired because of the costs."

I stroked Rudzia fluffy back.

"That's right," I began, "when it first broke down, I was twelve and I didn't want any other one. I searched the internet for schematics and fixed her with my DIY toolbox."

That really interested him. He put down his glass and leaned over to me.

"You fixed this little thing yourself?"

"It was nothing serious at the time. The power cell had a loose connection. It made me realize that something worse could happen, so I bought a virtual tech course and started learning."

"By yourself again..."

The doctor's peculiar tone of voice made me fully aware of something that I had not thought about before. Indeed, the interactive mentor-led training, consisting only of photons and an emotionally neutral voice, went smoothly and without turmoil. Problems arose only when I was dealing with real teachers and their methods, or worse, with the classroom.

"Yes," I admitted hesitantly. "The courses are well organized and nothing disturbed me in learning. And I was interested in DIY from an early age. Uncle Albert used to buy me DIY kits, and maybe that's why I got so into it."

"Have you gotten far? The same as dancing?"

"Well, maybe not as far, but I reached the academic level. I was very curious about everything that can be done with different tools."

My interlocutor jumped up briskly from his chair.

"Come on, let me show you something," he called.

He led me to a large annex at the back of the house, equipped with professional technical air conditioning – I immediately recognized it by the appearance of the outdoor unit. Residential buildings did not have such ones, instead using simple individual models. This one was not only to maintain the correct temperature inside, but also to filter the air and remove dust. The annex must have been something more, and indeed it was. Inside, I saw a workshop full of equipment that I could only dream of.

"Oh geez," I blurted out.

Even more interesting than the equipment, however, was the technical table on which someone was lying. Maybe something? I wasn't sure. The reclining figure looked like a young, dark-skinned woman with curly hair, but her chest was exposed, revealing a tangle of chips and relays. Another android. Admittedly, it looked like a piece of art.

"This is Raina," said Dr. O'Leary. "She broke down a few days ago. What is propeller pitch?" he asked suddenly.

"The theoretical distance that the propeller advances in one revolution moving through soft solid," I said reflexively.

"So we have theory down, too," he seemed to be very pleased. "Well, then how about something more complicated. What is Young's modulus?"

"I don't remember the exact definition, but it's used to determine the elasticity of the material."

"Very good. I see you have come a long way, even though you've only used virtual programs. Now for the practical part. Look at the parts on the other table and tell me something about them."

He sat down on a bench under the wall, leaned comfortably against the wall, and folded his arms over his chest.

I took Rudzia off my shoulder, sat her on the doctor's lap, and then obediently walked over to the indicated table. Something that lay on it didn't look like anything I knew at first glance. An openwork construction, bristling with numerous protrusions, and an element that, as I immediately thought, should fit inside. Both had traces of blackening. Encouraged by the doctor's gaze, I pushed across the counter an operational module of a technical macroscope much more advanced than the one I had brought from the shipment home for hobbyists. I synchronized the holographic lenses and immediately saw an increase in both parts. I took the largest of them with long tweezers.

"This is a cover, a sort of separator," I said after a moment. "It's made of a technical alloy, consisting of mostly platinum, as indicated by the weight and color of this scratch. I would venture to say that it was cast by the method of lost-wax casting. Whatever covers the surface is some kind of oxide. This is likely the result of high temperature, but the structure of the deposit indicates electrical overvoltage, not an open flame."

"Very well, go on" he encouraged me. I looked at him out of the corner of my eye. He smiled and carelessly stroked Rudzia in his lap.

"The same sediment is on the other side," I grabbed the smaller part with tweezers and adjusted the lenses. "I know what it is! It's a power dispenser responsible for distributing power to the servomotors. It's useless at the moment as the sludge acts as an insulator. It would have to be removed from both parts. They interact with each other and both should be equally functional."

"How would you do the cleaning?" O'Leary seemed very pleased with my answers.

"The separator with abrasive blasting first, with the smallest possible particle diameter. Then an acid bath and an ultrasonic bath and a thorough demagnetization before putting it in place.

The dispenser is much more fragile and, moreover, consists of several connected parts, so here you will have to clean it by hand. Precise and tedious work, but can still be done."

"Materials are in the drawer."

With the unpleasant feeling that I was passing some kind of exam, I opened the drawer and took out a set of cleaning products and brushes. I chose the manipulators and very carefully took the dispenser apart. I placed one of them in the micro-catcher, improved the focusing of the holo-lenses, soaked the brush with acid and got to work.

Dr. O'Leary watched me for a while and then suddenly said:

"Put it away. You'll finish another time."

"Excuse me?"

"I'm hiring you. You will be my assistant. You'll tell that to the employment center when you go there."

I was very surprised, but at the same time a stone fell from my heart. The thought that I would not have to depend on some official looking for a job for me was very reassuring.

"What about her?" I asked, nodding at Raina.

"I have the spare parts. In any case, we will finish repairing her together when you receive the official assignment," he sat Rudzia on his shoulder, walked over and looked at the deployed dispenser. "Nice. This little thing is some serious work, and you managed to unravel all the clues in less than a minute. You are good, you know that?"

I felt myself blush. The praise from the *doctor of androids* was undoubtedly valuable, but at the same time it caused me some embarrassment. I didn't feel like I deserved it. I played around with fixing different things from an early age, mainly thanks to Uncle Albert, who bought me more and more hobby kits – at first simple ones, then more and more advanced. I was able to develop my abilities thanks to him, which my mother knew well, but considered them completely unsuitable for a girl from a good family. Everything fell into one whole."

"My mom didn't want me to..."

The doctor suddenly stroked my head, like a small child's.

"Yes, I understand. You have to admit, she had a lot of right. If you were placed in a workers' district, you would have been trained according to your abilities and, who knows, you could even make a career there. That world is not some hell or a forced labor camp. It has its advantages, and after all, how would the world go on without workers? They are a fundamental social layer, Aura Maria. They play an extremely important role. It's true that you would be separated from your family, but other than that, you would not be hurt. You would grow up with the same people as you, and you would not need to feel inferior. But I understand your father's reluctance. Who knows, maybe I would do the same thing as he did."

"You don't know?"

"I don't have children. I don't know how it's like. But judging by how much the androids I work with mean to me; I can easily guess."

He looked at Raina. I did so too, but now I looked at her with a different gaze than before: she was supposed to be something like my patient. A really strange feeling, especially considering my complete ignorance when it comes to their psychology. However, they began to fascinate me, especially since I just saw what they have inside: a fascinating world of microcircuits that support the most important thing – an artificial brain. I had no idea what it could look like, but I was starting to feel respect towards it. At the same time, I was ashamed of the way I had treated Raul until now. As if he was just a bigger version of Rudzia. In the meantime, I began to realize that androids are more than a handful of processors, closed in the shape desired by the manufacturer.

"Is she conscious right now?" I asked quietly.

O'Leary shook his head.

"No. Androids can be put to sleep like a human, albeit in a different way, and this is called deactivation. She is currently unconscious. I guess it's hard to call it sleeping, because this state does not serve to regenerate, as it does in humans. I also don't know whether they dream. I mean, if they have something like a REM phase of the sleep, or the dreaming phase. There is no way to check."

"But... they could have them?"

"Well, who knows? You see, they have something of an internal life, although anthropocentrists deny that. It is a derived awareness of existence. They have preferences, a need to develop their skills, even something like aspirations. Generally speaking."

"Why 'generally speaking'?"

"Because she doesn't," he pointed at Raina, lying motionless like a doll. "This is a special case of halted development. During the most important period for an Android, she fell into the wrong hands with dire consequences. I have been taking care of her for many years, but I cannot repair the damage," he looked at me. "You're not going to ask why I'm wasting time on her in that case?"

I shook my head.

"No. I understand. You love her. Just like that. And when you love someone, there is no such thing as wasting your time."

He was silent for a while. Then he gave me a fatherly hug and kissed me on the cheek.

"You see, I was right. You are not stupid at all."

VIII

The employment office was located in Stone City. Up until now, exploring the surrounding areas, I have avoided this granite colossus, imagining how dark, cold and gloomy it must be inside. Of course, I was wrong, and I should have figured that out earlier, because who would choose to live in a dark cave with selection of well-equipped modular homes available on Celine Estate?

When I got there, it turned out that the inner part of the city looks like the interior of a huge shopping center. I couldn't see the living area because I didn't have a key card to access this section, but the rest was open and friendly to everyone. High corridors lit by 'eternal lamps', shopping strips with stores and entertainment venues. The office part was located in a place jokingly called *the attic,* that is, under the very peak of the mountain. The central elevator shaft, the only one of sufficient height, was carved into the heart of the mountain. It was glazed, so on the way up I could observe the neighboring floors of the city and what was happening on them. I gradually began to understand why people prefer to live here and not at Celine Estate. No one here seemed to be alone or abandoned. The townspeople worked together, went shopping together and played together, while in the neighborhood they rather avoided each other.

I found the employment office easily thanks to the clear diagram of the administrative area, located on the stand next to the elevator exit. It consisted of two rooms and a reception area, which at the moment was empty. Through the open door one could see a functionally arranged outer office, and even further a closed door to the office of the employment coordinator, dressed with a metal plate. There were diagrams on the walls that I didn't understand, abstract mosaic pictures and manual fire extinguishing equipment in three places. In the secretary's office, a young blond man was sitting behind a desk, typing on a computer.

I knocked on the doorframe. The clerk looked up and his round face lit up with a smile at the sight of me. At the same time, he blushed like a twelve-year-old girl caught watching social ads on the telenews by her friends. I recognized him immediately. This was the same boy who served newcomers in the office at the landing port and stared at me with such delight.

"So, you work here now?" I was surprised, before I even had time to think that it would be polite to at least say 'good morning'.

"I only work on the landing site on the arrival days," the man stood up and held out his hand to me. "Esteban Ponce. Friends call me Tebi."

"Aura Maria Solis," I shook his hand timidly. "Aurita for friends and family."

"Please, sit down. Are you here for work? We'll have to wait a bit, because the coordinator is out for lunch. Would you like some coffee?"

"Please."

I watched him brew local coffee and pour it into a cup. He was a little overweight, but still looked rather elegant. He clearly liked me, and I was flattered, especially since he made a positive impression on me. It's not the first time I've realized that being single at my age is not normal. But where would I have met someone before?

"Here you go," Esteban put a steaming cup and a plate of round cookies in front of me.

"Can I have some syrup, please. And... can we get on first name terms?" I suggested, not knowing where the impudence came from.

"I didn't have the courage to suggest so myself," he laughed nervously. "I'll be very pleased. I was wondering where you disappeared to, as you weren't in the city, and this is where all the other members of the new research team began living."

I took a sip of my coffee.

"I'm not part of the team," I explained, embarrassed. "It's a bit complicated. Actually, I was not supposed to be here, but a free spot appeared literally at the last moment, and I took the opportunity. I have family here."

"Solis... Solis... are you related to the twins?"

"I'm their niece."

He lit up even brighter than before.

"So, Estrella Solis, as well!"

"Did you know her?"

"Oh, yes. She was my first teacher. I should have immediately made the connection, as soon as I saw him with you," he pointed to Raul, who was standing at the door with an impenetrable expression, as usual. "That's her android. Did you inherit him?"

"In a manner. That was the decision of Aunt Estrella's daughter. He belonged to her, but she gave him to me."

Esteban took on a gloomier expression, as did Dr. O'Leary when his conversation turned to Jamie. What was the deal with this girl? I had the impression that nobody liked her.

"Etta wanted him to be free. To live life as he chooses to. She felt he deserved it, like any thinking creature. However, after her death, things got complicated."

I looked at Raul. What could he want? He was artificial, made in a factory, made for helping people. Could he really have desires of his own? I looked at him and could not imagine such a combination – logic circuits plus consciousness comparable to that of a human being, together with its strengths and weaknesses.

"Raul, what would you like to be doing if you could decide for yourself?" I asked after a while.

"It doesn't matter, Domina," he answered dryl. "I am an object by law, and I do not have a will of my own."

"Don't say that!" I protested, shocked by these words.

"Why? It's the truth."

The gentle innocence with which he spoke these words completely threw me off balance.

"Law this, law that... You are not a thing; you can think for yourself! I don't even feel that way about Rudzia. This is not fair!"

Esteban leaned over the table and laid a reassuring hand on my shoulder.

"Don't be angry, Aura. Unfortunately, Dr. Linde had a more conservative approach to android rights than Etta, and after her death, he decided that Raul would belong to Gemma. And since she gave him to you, he is yours now, and you're the one who decides."

I licked my lips.

"I don't want that. I mean, if he has other desires... I didn't know that he could have them. Raul, please say something."

He looked at me in silence, and it took me a while to realize that for him the word *something* was not something that could be understood in this context. He had some limitations, but after all, I had my own, too. I have known about that fir a long time. And yet, I didn't feel less human than others.

I tried again.

"What would you be doing if you didn't have to take care of me, and no one would command you?"

He tilted his head slightly.

"The hospital," he replied after a moment, awkwardly putting the words together: "Medicine. Nursing. Taking care of others. Sometimes I help doctors when I'm really needed, but only sometimes. Domina Estrella let me go there every day and be... a nurse."

"And what do the doctors say about it?"

"I think they were satisfied with my work. Except for Mr. Linde, who said I was too self-willed."

Esteban nodded in response to his words with a steady motion of his head.

"It's true," he said. "When my wife was dying, it was Raul who looked after her in the hospital. Linda tried to push him away, but she resisted him as much as she could, and then, eventually I objected, too."

"Why didn't Linde want Raul to be a nurse? What's wrong with that?" I couldn't understand the logic behind it.

"Because he is a humanist. He believes that androids *should know their place*. And that medicine must necessarily be closed to them, because people should take care of people, and artificial intelligence does not have the most important thing."

"What's that?"

"Empathy. Though he himself doesn't have much of it. When Veena was very ill, he offered her euthanasia instead of treatment. I almost punched him then."

I understood him well. I had terrible memories associated with that word too, and I didn't like it. I could not forget that on Earth they wanted to euthanize me.

"So, your wife died? I'm very sorry... but what was wrong with her?"

He sighed heavily and interlaced his fingers.

"When we were both children, she was stung by a mortal. It's one of the few local insect-like creatures. It's very poisonous. Veena needed a kidney transplant after the incident, and her mother became the donor. You know, we haven't had organ reserves here yet. Unfortunately, the donor's organ, even if it comes from someone blood-related and is compatible, often doesn't last as long as it should. Things got complicated when my wife got sick with a severe form of the Patrisian flu. Unfortunately, it was not possible to save her."

"That's so sad," I whispered.

"It has been six years already. We got married early. I was a fresh colonist, she was a local, that is, from the *Hawking Expedition*. She was already born here. She was eleven when we met, and I was ten. Now all I have left are memories of our beautiful love."

He spoke seriously, calmly, with nostalgia. I wanted to say something nice to him, but we both heard the clatter of high heels, and a middle-aged woman entered the office. Esteban jumped up from his chair, but she motioned her hand commandingly and slowly, as if in slow motion, he sat back down. I guessed that it must have been the coordinator.

The woman was plump but shapely, with a broad face and curly reddish hair. Although she was not particularly pretty, she seemed like she would be very popular with men. I don't know myself why such a thought occurred to me the moment I saw her. Maybe because she moved gracefully and looked like straight out of a magazine – although she was wearing simple clothes that resembled a uniform. Some women just are that way, even if they wrapped themselves in an old bag, they would still look admirable. And that's in the absence of classic features or an ideal figure. I immediately felt like a jagged peasant, although I was wearing my best blouse and freshly ironed pants.

The woman was plump but shapely, with a broad face and curly reddish hair. Although she was not particularly pretty, she seemed like she would be very popular with men. I don't know myself why such a thought occurred to me the moment I saw her. Maybe because she moved gracefully and looked like straight out of a magazine – although she was wearing simple clothes that resembled a uniform. Some women just are that way, even if they wrapped themselves in an old bag, they would still look admirable. And that's in the absence of classic features or an ideal figure. I immediately felt like a jagged peasant, although I was wearing my best blouse and freshly ironed pants.

"Oh, good morning," she said when she saw me. "I'm sorry I'm late. My name is Eva Svensson. Please, come to my office."

I finished my coffee hastily and stood up. I hoped that the coordinator would not notice my trembling hands and paleness, which I clearly saw when I looked in the mirror on the wall along the way. Esteban was silent, he didn't even move."

"No, Raul, stay," I forced myself to order the android, which was going to follow me.

Svensson gestured to a chair and closed the door. She herself sat down at a table of gleaming polished wood.

"So, you were included in the list of an additional group of technicians as Master Alma Jablonsky," she began, looking at the transparent computer screen. "However, already during the flight we received a message that the real Jablonsky remained on Earth, and you've illegally taken her place. Do you plead guilty?"

"Yes," I replied. "I took advantage of the fact that there was a free hibernation capsule and..."

"Don't treat me like an idiot," she interrupted me sharply. "We're talking about bribery of public officials, hacking of the federal computer and falsification of data. Of course, these are not your crimes, but you used them to get here."

I made the most apologetic face I could. To my quiet surprise, I was no longer afraid, I was just a little tense. Something in me was clearly changing, and I liked it.

"At first I was furious," Svensson continued, "there are certain rules in this colony and it is definitely not a haven for the unadapted. But then they sent me your complete dossier, and I understood it a little. Your father fought against the entire world so that you could lead a good life... so that you could live at all, because you were threatened with physical elimination from society. It's a great example of parental love and has made me a little more sympathetic towards you. But my best intentions won't help much if you are useless to the colony. So what can you do?"

I coughed in embarrassment and laid a piece of computer foil on the table.

„This is Dr. O'Leary's statement," I said quietly. "He agreed to hire me in his workshop as an assistant and secretary. I am good with all kinds of tools and have an eidetic memory. I will be useful to him.

Svenson raised her well-groomed eyebrows, then unrolled the foil and began reading. After a moment, she nodded.

"That makes it easier," she said with obvious relief. "I can now, with a clear conscience, put you on the list of colonists who receive allowance and monthly wages for their work in the community. I was really troubled about what I would do with you.

It wasn't hard to believe. Her role was definitely not easy, and my case could cost her a few gray hairs. This was definitely not something this woman dealt with every day. But what was the complete message from Earth?

"Miss Svensson, did they say anything else about my father in what they sent you?" I asked with trembling heart.

She looked at me over the keyboard.

"Are you worried about him? You have a reason to, since everything came out. But no, they didn't mention anything. Such data is not related to the colony."

"How could I learn something?"

She pushed away from the computer and rested her elbows on the table.

"You can't," she said dryly. "I advise you to not even make any signs of you being here, otherwise we both will have problems."

"What do you mean, we both will?" I didn't understand.

"Because in the first message I was told to send you back without even opening the hibernator. I went with it to the Solis twins, demanding an explanation. Then they told me what you threaten you and why your father decided to break the law so harshly. And I, the stupid woman I am, was moved and started thinking about it. I made a decision. The dossier sent to me later only convinced me of it."

"So, what did you do?" I gasped out.

"After receiving the protocol of picking up the hibernation capsules from the deck of the ship, I falsified the data and transmitted to Earth that the Alma Jablonski's hibernator was damaged before takeoff due to incorrect programming, probably by an unauthorized person. And the still unknown woman who was riding in it died."

I looked at her with rounded eyes, not understanding anything.

"Why? Why did you take such a risk? You don't even know me."

She leaned back in her chair.

"That's true," she admitted calmly. "I don't know you, but at the same time, I do. On Earth, I was a social controller. Back then, I believed I was doing the right thing, but here... here I began looking at things differently. Do you know what lies at the heart of our family code and all the tough decisions that come with it?"

I shook my head in silence, not taking my eyes off her.

"Overpopulation, which has plagued humanity for several centuries, even before the ecological catastrophe. This, and only this. The disaster has led to a sharp decline in supplies of clean water and food. Some decisions had to be made, ones which at some points were unthinkable. And that's how it works even today. But Patris is not Earth. The conditions are different here, and here you can see something we don't pay attention to on our home planet."

I didn't know what she was talking about and didn't have the courage to ask. Not waiting for my reaction, she cleared her throat and continued without encouragement.

"Estrella Solis knew this before, as did others like her. However, they did nothing about it, because how would they? Here we were given a chance to restore what humanity had lost on the way to stabilization after the catastrophe. To a relative well-being. But not everyone likes that."

"Not everyone?" I repeated thoughtlessly.

"The fact that the colony is governed by laws other than those imposed by earthly society alarmed the authorities. They decided to act."

I felt cold. There was something in her voice that was frightening, or maybe I was imagining it?

"Is it dangerous?" I let out.

"Whatever we could say about it, Patris is an Earth colony. So it claims the rights to it. We got a tip from... a kind man that the last transport will bring the people who are supposed to take power here."

That's just my luck!

"And did they?" I asked breathlessly.

Eve Swenson laughed heartily.

"No, of course not. Not yet. They wouldn't risk anything as long as they're wearing the surveillance bracelets. But they were disabled today. Yours did too, didn't it?"

Truth. The bracelet fell from my left ankle this morning. I put it in my purse and completely forgot about it. I took it out and examined it carefully.

"It's not without reason that I invited you today specifically. Of all Hyamdal adult passengers, only you are not suspicious for obvious reasons. Although, of course, we couldn't rule out double coverage."

"I don't understand," I admitted. My head was spinning.

"I mean that you were offered to us as a mentally retarded fugitive, when in fact you are an agent who is meant take my place with the support of soldiers," she explained. "But if that was the case, you would not have come here today. You would have gone to a completely different place."

"What makes you so sure?"

"Because..." Mrs. Svensson didn't finish speaking when we heard a dull rumble from the hallway, followed by shouting and stamping of feet. We jumped up from our seats. Svensson pressed the button that opened the door between the office and the secretary's office.

Everything happened in a split second. First thing I saw was Raul, holding someone in a professional chokehold while Esteban was desperately trying to activate his desktop communicator. Then two soldiers aimed their firearms at us through the open office door. I didn't even have time to get scared when the android pushed the held person with such force that his body dully slammed against the attackers, knocking them off the floor. Shots rang out, but they reached the ceiling, and the next moment Raul pulled the weapon out of the hands of the surprised soldiers. They were well trained – they immediately launched a counterattack, trying to immobilize the android and take the rifles from him.

"Security, code red! I repeat, code red in office number six!" Esteban shouted into the communicator's microphone.

Then he jumped out from behind the table, grabbed a fire extinguisher from the wall and directed a stream of frosty foam from the diffuser at the attackers. A scream filled the room.

I stood as if rooted to the floor, not knowing what to do. Oddly enough, the only thing I was thinking about now was that these soldiers would need urgent help. The reactive foam used to extinguish fires causes deep frostbite due to a strong endothermic reaction, and that's nothing surprising. Its action can even break metal, let alone a human body. The foam-covered metal of the rifles must have been burning the soldiers like acid, and they couldn't be rid of them, because the cold burned the muscles of the arms, and the frozen metal stuck to their skin.

Svennsen, standing next to me, pressed a button on her desk.

"We need the medical team, room six," she ordered calmly. When she finished, the guards called by her secretary appeared.

"I'm sorry, Your Excellency, we were stopped," a large man in uniform with the insignia of a major apologized in a breathless voice.

"It's fine, Sherman. Who could have known that they would right away want to hit two places at once and that they would do it by force?"

"Excellency?!" I looked at Svensson with widened eyes. She smiled slightly.

"I am the governor of the colony," she explained frivolously. "I beat four other candidates during the last election."

Beat?

"Did you fight?" I asked in horror. In my imagination I saw a huge ring, inside which..."

Svensson struggled to suppress his laughter.

"No, not like that. I defeated them in the elections. More people voted for me than others."

"Ah," I finally realized. I don't know what came to my mind... "I'm sorry, I'm stupid.

"No, you're not, just a little naive. And that's not a crime," she patted me on the back.

This is the second person who told me something of the like. Maybe I really wasn't as worthless as the officials from the social commission claimed?

"My teachers said that democratic elections are an outdated method that is not used today as it doesn't give the best results," I recalled. "Sometimes even tragic results."

One of my home-schooling teachers was a big fan of political science and often gave me lectures on the matter. He talked about the lies of politicians, smear campaigns and the propaganda of success, about a whole network of media aimed at manipulating the minds. It was very interesting, and I remembered a lot of it, unlike other lessons.

"It's true," Svensson agreed. "But we have improved the formula a little. The colonists evaluate the candidates' achievements and their predisposition to performing public functions, while the rivals themselves don't have any say. During the campaign, they are not allowed to even talk to the rest of the citizens. Not to anybody."

Very interesting. I knew that since a long time ago, on Earth, individual government officials are elected by a computer that objectively assessed their suitability for office, and that this method works better than anything that humanity has invented so far. However, the colonists abandoned this efficient system in favor of direct elections. Did this worry the Earth to such an extent that they sent forces to seize power by force?

"What now?" I watched as the medics put the groaning soldiers on the stretchers.

"Now I will be interrogating our prisoners," Svensson headed toward the door. "I'm going back to my duties, and the real coordinator, Corey Frank, will take care of you. I had to ensure in person that you are not a government agent. That's why I put on this masquerade. For now, go home and rest. You'll need it," she paused, looked at the android and squeezed his hand lightly. "Thank you, Raul. If it weren't for you, a very dangerous situation might have arisen."

That's true, it might have. Now I realized that Raul's lightning-fast reaction somehow didn't fit in with the idea that androids are generally incapable of improvising. He clearly was. He reacted not only extremely quickly, but also in a way that allowed him to assume his own assessment of the entire situation. Yet again, he surprised me. I was beginning to understand why Aunt Estrella wanted him to be free. He really did act like a human being. And a human being shouldn't be the property of another person.

IX

Only later did I learn the behind the scenes of the failed coup d'état in the colony. Fortunately, there were only three wounded, two from the colony and one of the arrived troops, not counting, of course, those whom Esteban treated with the fire extinguisher. After an exchange of official diplomatic notes with headquarters on Earth, it was decided that the entire incident was due to a misunderstanding – Lieutenant Smith, commander of the unit, misinterpreted the received orders. Or so they say. Even I wouldn't believe that, but it was polite and safer to pretend that we all bought into it. I felt sorry for this young lieutenant. I would bet all my movable assets that he would be turned into a scapegoat, even if he was acting on official orders. I knew from television programs that this is how the political world works, and that's how it has been for millennia.

The colony council decided to put all the participants in the conspiracy – the soldiers and four civilians – in hibernation capsules and leave them there, awaiting the next ship from Earth. It was decided that later they would be handed over to the ship's crew for transportation to our home planet. I was unable to find out who specifically shared the information of what was happening. The Governor kept this message to herself, of course, not in vain. She must have counted on further messages from her agent. In any case, that shouldn't interest me. I was now a girl working for her own livelihood, an independent person – something the public committee would never have believed. I wish they could see me now.

After my first month of work, I invited myself to join Kenneth Linda and his wife for a Sunday lunch. I needed to talk to them about Raul. His matter didn't give me peace, and the android's silent obedience drove me to despair. It didn't bother me that much before, but when I realized how human-like he was, it felt wrong. Very wrong. I felt it especially now when I was working with Dr. O'Leary to get Raina back to normal. Until now, the doctor has entrusted me with simple tasks, mainly cleaning small parts and installing them on modules, from which they didn't come from, as well as keeping records of our work. As he explained to me, busy with his current work, he didn't have time to do so until now, and he didn't want to introduce someone random into his little kingdom.

"I've had an assistant once before," he said, putting new pieces into Raina's chest. He did it by hand, without using manipulators with appropriate programming. "His name was Leonard Derkach. Unfortunately, he died tragically while exploring the Sea of Terror."

"Brr," I shivered. "It sounds awful just by the name. Why *Sea of Terror*?"

"Because it's dangerous," he replied seriously. "It's best to not even get close to it, let alone explore it. Patris is by no means a garden of delight, although at first glance one could be fooled."

I looked up from my work.

"I think it's beautiful."

"Because it is. But it's also very dangerous. Many of us died before we learned to avoid threats and live-in harmony with this planet."

The doctor became not only my first employer, but also my mentor. That was supposed to be Raul's role, but he only answered questions. And I didn't always know what to ask. O'Leary just talked, told me stories, and he did it in such an interesting way that I listened to him with great interest. Sometimes his wife Astrid would join us. We immediately became friends. Lieutenant Astrid turned out to be a really sweet, joyful person who loves the whole world, and therefore me as well. That was another change in my life, because I've never had friends before.

During this time, I had made a male friend – Esteban Ponce (a funny last name, now that I think about it) called several times and finally invited me for a short walk. It soon became clear that he was not turned away by my low IQ, which I immediately admitted to him. I hate lying and avoiding the truth, I believe that it could ruin any relationship between people.

"The regular IQ tests don't say anything about a person," he commented my confession. "I don't care if you can calculate pi to the eight power or if your mathematical abilities end at the multiplication table. Veena couldn't solve even a simple equation of analytic geometry, and I loved her like crazy. You are beautiful as you are, with your strengths and weaknesses."

This approach to assessing the value of a person was new to me. All my earthly experiences show that a member of society is worth as much as they can give to society. And this, in turn, depended on their skills and ability to fulfill the tasks assigned to them. Here at Patris, they thought differently. When did these people learn this? After all, everyone except those born here came from Earth. They have undergone extensive training and have been tested several times. Before leaving, they were a social elite. What changed?

I can't deny that it was all above me. Until now, I didn't realize how important Earth's laws were to me, even though they pushed me to the margins of society. Despite the painful feeling of such discrimination, I was surrounded by a sense of security, immutable rules. Almost everything was different here. The colony developed its own moral code literally in the first years of its existence. It was like a passive rebellion, so it's not surprising that the Earthly authorities became concerned. After all, Patris was not settled – with enormous effort and expenditures – so that the people there would regress in social development. They were to set the stage for what could be called *Earth 2.0* in case more people would need to be evacuated from their home planet. Meanwhile, they created a small country that wanted to have its own rules. This couldn't please their leaders.

Initially, I was tormented by the absurdly naive thought that the Earth could send warships here to force obedience. Later, however, when I discovered Aunt Estrella's personal files, I laughed at the idea. The Earth didn't have cosmic warships, as they do in movies for teenagers. All space missions were peaceful, because there was simply no one to fight with. It would take a lot of time and resources to build a battleship equipped with the right weapons, and it would be pointless. The creation of a fleet of such ships was ruled out for economic and logistical reasons, even I knew about that, and a single ship bristling with cannons like a porcupine would be all too obvious of a target. The colony had an observatory that could easily detect an approaching ship early enough to prepare for defense, and long-range scanners that could classify its weapons.

That was not all. My aunt also wrote that somewhere near Stone City there are several air defense systems. She didn't know where exactly, but I believed her that they existed. If I would have made the choice to install them, then so would Governor Svensson and those who ruled here before her. After all, they knew that by changing the rules, they were putting themselves in danger from Earth. According to aunt's notes, they thought it over very carefully and nevertheless took the risk. An important role in this was played by her friend Veronica Hornet, the first official coordinator of the colony, appointed by the then governor and commander of the garrison Sasha Krasusky. However, my aunt also participated in the work on Patris's first constitution and helped to loosen the laws on childbirth. That's what bothered Earth the most.

The colonists didn't seem like the kind of people who would surrender without a fight. And a fight would mean death and destruction. One side will end up the winner, but for what purpose? The colony was valuable only when it functioned; if destroyed, it would have no value. Thus, a forceful solution had to be ruled out, on the other hand, I knew that the Earth would not give up its demands. And Patris absolutely needs regular supplies, so a compromise had to be found. A difficult situation. I was really glad that it wasn't me who had to figure it out.

On Sunday I put on my best clothes and went to Dr. Linde's house. In addition to the couple, I also came across Jamie there, who had just returned from camp, tanned to a bronze, slimmer and probably taller as well. As soon as I entered, she hugged me and kissed me for all times.

"Aura Maria, you have no idea how wonderful it was!" she said cheerfully as Tina Roberts laid out the plates on the table. "What have you been doing the entire summer? I already heard that you have a job, congratulations. But what else?"

"I explored the area," I said honestly. "I also learned a lot about this planet and the colony. You know, from the computer. If I am going to study, I prefer to do it on my own."

"Did Raul not help you?"

"When something was not clear, I asked him. But he's rather quiet, you know."

She grimaced slightly.

"I know. That's what's annoying about him. I bet you're getting tired of him already, huh?"

Before I could answer, Tina Roberts spoke.

"Girls, wash your hands and sit down at the table. You can talk then."

"What's for dinner tonight?" Jamie instantly forgot about Raul.

"Baked dunlin legs, carrot puree and young potatoes with lard. What you like best," smiled Tina. Her usually stern face softened. She must have loved her adopted daughter dearly, definitely more than my mother ever loved me.

"You have earthly potatoes here?" I asked to drive away the sad thoughts.

I wasn't yet aware of how varied the local menu was. Over the past month, I've been eating mostly prepared protein foods, rarely tasting anything else. I didn't quiet believe in the culinary abilities of my android, so I used ready-made *iron portions* that were filling my closet to the brim. Most of them were from Aunt Estrella's days, but they were still edible. They didn't require much preparation, but they did their job. My father and my uncle ran, as they say, a *bachelor estate*, neither of them knew how to cook, so I learned to see food as something necessary and nothing else. So, it was all the easier for me to be content with the protein cubes and fruits that grew on the trees around the estate, which everyone was allowed to harvest.

"Yes," said miss Roberts. "It's a very resilient and fertile plant, it can adapt anywhere. I've heard that it even grew on the barren sands of Mars, although this may be an urban legend. One way or another, it was the first thing that was planted here, and it produced crops without any issues."

"What about the carrots?" I asked.

"They are a bit like earthly carrots, but sweeter and sharper. You'll see."

Dr. Linde entered the dining room, buttoning his shirt on the way.

"I hope I didn't oversleep? Hello, Aurita," he kissed me on the cheek. "I'm glad you finally remembered about us."

I was confused.

"I didn't want to intrude," I muttered.

"Nonsense. What do you mean, intrude? In a sense, we are family. You will always be welcome here."

Well, let's just say... I didn't feel those family ties, even *in a sense*. But well, if he says so, then let him be."

Tina served dinner and we began eating. As befits well-mannered people, they ate in silence, and the conversation began only after dessert – tiny fruit cookies and strong coffee with whipped cream.

"So, how are you liking our colony?" the doctor asked me.

"It's very beautiful," I said. "And I think it's very well organized. I walked around the entire estate and surveyed the surroundings. Raul showed me the recreation centers, the hospital, the workshop... everything that was worth seeing."

"So, I'm guessing that he's useful to you?"

Jamie laughed a little, drawing her foster father's scolding gaze.

I took another cookie to keep my hands busy.

"I wanted to talk about him with you."

Linde raised his pale eyebrows.

"Is something wrong?"

"No, that's not what I mean," I took a bite of the cookie. "I know that Raul sometimes helps at the hospital. Couldn't he do that regularly?"

The doctor and his wife looked at each other.

"Is he troubling you?"

"No, that's not it. Has it ever occurred to you that he might have his own wants?"

Tina Roberts sighed.

"We could have guessed that it would eventually come to this. You resemble Etta too much... not necessarily physically, of course, but in reactions, in the way you think. She, too, felt that we were treating androids unfairly. Only that, you see, the situation is not so unambiguous and simple."

"Androids lack imagination, spontaneity in action," Linde butted in again. "They need to be supervised. Idealists like Etta and Mac O'Leary don't consider the importance of the ability to make impulsive decisions in life. For us, that is something natural, like breathing, but for them it's completely inaccessible. They would not be able to survive in an unpredictable environment, unlike humans."

There was a lot of truth in what he said, I knew that, but I persisted.

"Nevertheless, I think that Raul could still work in the hospital, as he really likes that job. After all, there are medical androids."

Linde shook his head desperately.

"I see you still don't understand. Medical androids have a medical program applied to them during the manufacturing process. Companion androids don't. Raul can be very helpful, I don't deny that, but only when supervised. And there is not always time and opportunity for such supervision."

"Tell her everything," Jamie said. She leaned back in her chair and sipped water and juice through a straw. As I noticed, she avoided coffee. "Let her know that this is not our, so to speak, narrow-mindedness."

Intrigued, I looked at the doctor. He seemed confused and embarrassed. He rubbed his freckled nose with his finger and tried to find the right words.

"I know how you feel, Aurita. I like Raul too. However, we shouldn't be misguided by our feelings. For a time, Raul was a good MA, short for *Medical Android*. In truth. It was my fault. I gave him too much freedom, I trusted him too much, perhaps carried away by Etta's enthusiasm. She always wanted to treat androids as equals, and she encouraged others to do so."

"What happened?" I encouraged him to continue when he fell silent.

"One time, there was an accident at the hospital. One of the fire barriers slammed shut due to an emergency. It shut down the infirmary while one of our researchers, Miranda Olivares, was there. She came to donate blood. She was nine months pregnant at the time. The falling fences caused a tremor, making one of the hanging cabinets fall down at Miranda's head. The girl lost consciousness, and contractions began at the same time. Raul wasn't able to help her. Communications were cut and no one was there to direct him. A human being would at least try to deliver the baby, to do anything at all. Maybe he could've done something. It was not a complicated birth... but Raul did nothing. He just stood there and watched, because he knew nothing about such things and he had nowhere to get this knowledge."

"What happened?" I whispered.

"They both died. Miranda and her little son. When the ambulance team finally made it to the infirmary, they found them dead, and Raul still stood motionless like a statue. He only said that *they stopped functioning*. He was confused and couldn't handle it. A man in his place would have acted instinctively. That's not something an android has, so he failed. Do you understand now?"

I understood him very well. It became a lot clearer to me.

"That's really awful. What did you do?"

"Nothing," Tina quickly assured me. "It was not Raul's fault, but it made us realize that an android cannot go beyond certain limits, just like a person cannot learn to fly without artificial means. It's just that from that day on we are more careful and don't put on androids' shoulders more than they can carry."

I had no idea how to answer that. I felt that Linde was right and wrong at the same time, and I could not find the right words.

"But you blame him for what happened," I muttered at last as the silence stretched out.

"No. I know I was the one at fault. I was the director of the hospital. Chief physician. I shouldn't have let the android stand alone in the infirmary," the doctor shivered. "Let's not talk about this anymore. If you care about this so much, I can hire Raul as an assistant of a nurse on the condition that under no circumstances should he be left alone with a patient. But how will you manage then?"

"Oh, uncle!" Jamie looked up. "Sometimes you say such things that... Aunt Aura is not a baby! She doesn't need a nanny to wipe her nose. She can handle herself."

"Keep your nose out of this, kid. Do you remember what the twins said?"

"Yes, I do. So what? They didn't really say anything that serious, you two just keep telling yourself something. You've convinced yourselves that the twins will lay on our heads some kind of underdeveloped victim of fate that can't even use the bathroom by herself," the girl sped up and didn't even pay attention to her foster mother's hissing," Aura Maria is not stupid at all, because If she was, O'Leary would never have hired her in his studio! How many applications did he get after Derkach's death? Ten? Fifteen? He didn't want to introduce anyone to his world. And he accepted her right away, even though she doesn't even have a master's degree, let alone a doctorate. Hah, she can't even brag about a bachelor's degree. She must be really good."

I raised my hand in protest.

"That's not how it is."

"Then how is it?" she looked at me in bewilderment.

"I think McLean O'Leary needed a skilled and obedient assistant, not an ambitious graduate student who would act like a smartass with him at every opportunity. That's why I caught his attention, or rather, he made a decision during our conversation, when I told him how I learned from educational programs."

"You're self-taught?" Tina was clearly surprised. They must really have thought I was a complete idiot.

"Yes. I was much better at learning from virtual instructors than from living teachers. Studying precise mechanics, I achieved the academic level and almost made it to the bachelor degree level when the social commission tracked me down."

Now Linde opened his mouth in amazement and for a moment looked at me with widened eyes, as if at a miracle.

"Are you serious?"

"Of course. It can be checked with virtual registers, I'm sure you have access here. All my achievements were officially registered in the registers of the Technical University. Either way, you could just ask me questions or make me fix something."

"Amazing," he scratched absently at the back of his head, still looking at me. "Could have the department of genetics and social control been this wrong about you? How is that even possible with the present state of science? And nobody even thought about it?"

"The results of virtual learning cannot influence the assessment of the community commission," his wife explained. "They are too easily fabricated."

I shrugged and ate another cookie. They were quite delicious.

"They weren't entirely wrong," I said, "I have problems, I admit. O'Leary called them social dysfunction. I can neither study in a group, nor take exams in the presence of strangers. I quite literally freeze up and I'm unable to function. There is no way to fix that. When there was only me and the virtual teacher, who never lost patience and whom I could turn off at any moment, I managed. The official IQ tests are like black magic for me. I don't know why, and nobody does, not even O'Leary can explain it for sure. He claims that some part of my brain is not functioning properly and that this is more likely the result of an illness than some kind of congenital defect. However, as you can see, I can manage."

I smiled at the house owners. To my surprise, I was not angry with them, I felt sorry for them. I'm sure the fact that they would have to take care of me was extremely unfavorable for them, and they still felt uncomfortable in my presence.

"You don't have to apologize to me," I continued as they exchanged helpless glances while the disagreeable Jamie held back her laughter. "I understand your objections. The uncles never saw me, they only knew the scraps of reality that my father gave them. They probably also thought that I was underdeveloped, like a babbling child. They only agreed to take care of me because of their older brother…"

"That's not true," my cousin argued vigorously. "They only said that you were *a little special*. And you are true, but I really like you. The old AI man does too, as we can see, and that one's pretty damn picky."

"Jamie..." Tina moaned helplessly.

"What? I'm just saying the truth."

"That's enough," Linde interrupted the upcoming quarrel and turned to me. "Forgive us our distance to you, Aura Maria. We just didn't know what to expect, and so we decided that Raul's care would be the best way out of the situation. In truth, we never really planned for Jamie to live with you, we just made it seem that way."

"You were afraid of me," I whispered.

It was a logical conclusion, and it was quite understandable. I was well aware that in the past, people with mental disorders and even mentally ill were just a part of society, which led to many unfortunate events. All the more, doctors and policemen knew about it. They could imagine literally everything.

"Well, maybe we weren't *afraid*. We just didn't know what to expect. If someone is secretly raising a child hidden from the Regional Social Commission and then bribes the school board, they must have serious reasons."

"We managed to forget how strict the criteria for reproduction and upbringing on Earth are," Tina Roberts rejoined. "And how little it takes to cross off a child. I hope that you can understand us."

I nodded slightly. I did understand them. I felt a little sorry about it, I admit, but only a little bit. Indeed, they could have felt threatened if their imaginations ran wild.

"How about you finish this boring conversation," Jamie yawned unexpectedly. "Aura Maria, autumn is coming and the season of games is about to begin. Will you come cheer for my team?"

I looked at her in a semi-conscious state.

"Yes, of course... what do you play?"

"What else? Chess! I told you already that I spent the summer at a sports camp!"

I must have looked confused because Linde hastened to explain:

"It's not the kind of chess that you think. In any case, when the tournaments begin, you will see for yourself. This is the most popular entertainment here."

"As for entertainment, tomorrow is a holiday," Tina intervened, delighted to change the awkward topic. "First Landing Day, do you have any plans?"

I felt myself blush.

"Ah, yes," I admitted hesitantly. "Esteban Ponce invited me for a hike in the mountains and a picnic."

"Benito..." I added silently. Colleagues and friends called him that. I really liked the diminutive, it suited Esteban. In general, I have always liked all diminutives, and they were widely used at my home. They called me Aurita or Rita. Uncle Albert called my father Johnny, instead of Jonathan, and my father called uncle Tito. When things weren't so bad between my parents, he called my mother Nena. To utter a full name meant a serious conversation or a reprimand.

In fact, Esteban called me almost every day after we met at the work coordinator's office. Not that he was imposing himself – he asked before that whether I mind. I agreed without hesitation. For obvious reasons, no one has ever made any moves towards me before, and I really liked this change. Esteban was not the only one. Since I started working regularly, I stopped hiding at Aunt Estrella's house, and the local young people began noticing me. Their gazes the courtesies they threw at me scared me at first, but I quickly learned to enjoy them. At last, I felt like a bird released from the cage in which it had spent its entire life.

Everything here was different than on Earth. There was no social control. Nobody wondered if you had the S-card, assuring your mental health. They didn't check your hours at the compulsory gym. Also, there were no rules for compulsory sexual intercourse for 'health reasons. On the other hand, if two people wanted to get married, no one bothered them, even if they belonged to different reproductive fitness classes. The only thing that was strictly observed was social supervision over the upbringing of children. They were considered the colony's greatest treasure – for good reason, since childbearing was still too rare. In the hospital, they fought for each one who had at least a minimal chance of survival, and therefore one day I stumbled upon a girl with obvious features of congenital dwarfism. She was treated with hormones and rehabilitated, which wouldn't have happened on Earth. She simply wouldn't have been born.

"Ah, you mean Camille Lefevre," smiled Dr. O'Leary when I told him about the meeting. "You see, her example proves what was said by Etta, Veronika Hornet and doctor Villard, who initiated the pregnancy and neonatal protection program. The kid is incredibly talented, has an excellent memory, sings beautifully and writes poetry. None of the other kids here can do that. The Malthusian education of a healthy society was costly. According to the architects of the new order, it was worth the price. I'm not so sure about that."

I believed it was not. I've been told this before, but after spending eight to ten hours every day with O'Leary, I discovered that he was an eccentric. He had his own views on everything and loved to talk about them for hours, and since I listened and didn't stop him, we had a good time working together. He gave me more and more difficult tasks, and I coped with all of them. Thanks to this, I gained courage and confidence in myself, less and less often thought about the Earth. I gradually began to think of Patris as my homeland, even though I didn't fully know it yet.

X

Esteban Ponce lived right in the middle of the estate. He occupied a two-section house surrounded by a small garden full of earthly roses. The gates were open, so I entered without hesitation and immediately regretted it. By the time I realized, I was lying on the ground. Something suddenly attacked me – something terrible, winged, bald and toothy, knocking me off my feet like a wild cat with its prey. It occurred to me that this was probably the last second of my life. The reptile's mouth was right next to my face, but instead of crushing my skull with its mighty mouth, it only made a sound resembling a very loud rustle. Then the creature stuck out its split tongue and happily licked my nose.

"Firefly, come here!" I heard Esteban's voice. "I'm sorry, Aura Maria, I forgot to tell you. This is Weena's harpoid, he lives with me. A local animal, quite intelligent and gets attached quickly."

Apologizing profusely, he pulled the obviously amused creature away from me, grabbing the collar on its long, thin neck.

"It's f-fine," I grumbled, standing up and brushing myself off from the sand. My heart was pounding like crazy, I was scared, but looking at the harpoid now, I realized that it was a really tame creature and simply wanted to play.

I defiantly put my hand to my chest. The harpoid hissed softly again, tilting his scaly head. He blinked his white eyes and widened his mouth in a parody of a smile. I patted him hesitantly on the back, just above the wings.

"Good boy."

"Now that you two have met, we will take him with us, if you don't mind. Harpoids are very affectionate and don't like being left alone at home."

"What about when you go to work?"

"I take him then, too. He sleeps in the closet next to the office, and I visit him during breaks. He is very well-behaved."

I laughed, now completely disarmed. This strange pet seemed to me repulsive, funny and cute at the same time. I also understood why Esteban was so attached to him. If he was his only companion after his wife's death, then who could blame him? I knew very well what loneliness is and how important having any sort of company is. Even imaginary ones, or ones working on microcircuits.

We took a trip in the *clog*, as they commonly called the solar cars made from local materials. I already knew they weren't perfect. Most of all rather slow and heavy. The wood obtained from the Patrisian 'water trees', powerful whole-stemmed plants, is very cohesive, fine-celled and, even after careful drying, contains a high percentage of water. As I heard from Dr. O'Leary, the phenomenon of these trees is their building block – in their molecules, carbon is replaced by silicon, which binds water in the form of a gel, so that the water trees can grow anywhere. From time to time, after absorbing water, they store it in the form of a gel and use it as needed, and they can take huge amounts. A moisturized earthen tree usually starts to rot, while this one turns the liquid into a gel and stores it for later without any harm to itself.

The unique structure of water trees makes the wood obtained from them resilient, highly resistant and, above all, non-combustible. Their only drawback is their weight density and the fact that water trees were not as common as people would like them to be. Most of the plants on Patris are carbonaceous, just like on Earth. Few use silicon as a base, and scientists are wondering how such duality is possible in one biological niche. The engineers didn't care. They were happy that they were able to build comfortable cars from this material, accessible to every inhabitant of the colony, and that's all that mattered.

For the location of our picnic, Esteben chose a spot at the foot of the Wavy Mountains, where the Patris's most beautiful flowers are said to grown and edible fruits of various varieties ripened. It was called *Little Paradise* and was a favorite meeting place for the entire community, but only during the summer months when the weather was favorable.

"People still come there right now, so you'll probably meet a few people," he said. "It's time, you can't be constantly isolated like that. You'll become a weirdo from it, and that would be a pity.

Such a beautiful and kind girl should shine in others' company, not hide in the corners."

"You know, I'm not very good at making friends," I muttered.

"I'll help you," he suggested, adding a little speed.

Curled up at my feet, Firefly hissed. I felt him shiver. Encouraged by an incomprehensible flash of intuition, I looked around and saw a gray-brown mass rising above the horizon.

"Benito!" I shouted. "What is that?!"

Esteban glanced in the rearview mirror.

"Oh, damn," he cursed. "That's a living storm! Forecasters didn't mention it, and it's a month ahead of schedule... we can expect a difficult autumn."

"What is a *living storm*?" I didn't understand. It sounded intimidating. Harpoid, pressed to my feet, squeaked uneasily.

"You'll probably understand why we call it that if you take a closer look. Now hold on, I need to put as much heat as much as the factory supplied," with these words, he pressed on the gas pedal all the way. The vehicle rushed forward with a powerful spring.

I continued looking around. The thunderous mass chasing us continued to grow and darken, gradually becoming almost black with gray-yellow accents. Suddenly it swelled up, and a huge, terrible, twisted face with an open mouth flew out of it, as if about to scream. I jerked back and screamed in fear as hard as my lungs allowed.

"Relax! It won't hurt you. We can escape it."

"Who is that? What is that?" I blurted out, trembling with fear. I cowered, trying to hide behind the backrest and back seat cushion. I instinctively hugged Firefly, and he immediately pressed against me. He was afraid, too, and it was easy to understand why. From the direction of the turbulent whirlpool, we could hear a growing howl and roar, although rather weak, but becoming louder. For the animal's sensitive hearing, this must have been terrible.

"It's not a creature. It's just an illusion. It's a specific type of sandstorm," Esteban explained to me. "It carries away everything that it can: soil, small pebbles, dead leaves, branches... all of that creates micro-swirls in the air that distribute the density of the material in a specific way. If you look from far enough, you can see that face... but it is in fact not there. This phenomenon is called pareidolia. Our brain recognizes a face in everything it sees, as it is programmed by nature. Some even see how hands reach out to them, but it is still only a storm. A common natural phenomenon."

"Common, sure…" I muttered. I still couldn't take my eyes off the gruesome face that stubbornly followed in our footsteps. It almost filled the horizon, giving the impression that it was about to catch us and swallowed us whole. „What if it catches up with us?"

"It won't. One of the storm shelters should be around here, „Esteban said calmly, even frivolously. "They are spread out around the estate and anywhere people go. Living storms are not very strong, but you better not get caught in the middle of one.

What they carry with them acts like sandpaper on biological tissues, so if it ever catches you by surprise in an open space, lie on your stomach, cover your face with your clothes, and lie still until it passes. You are usually relatively safe close to the ground."

That somehow didn't calm me down at all. Fortunately, after a while Esteban shouted joyfully and turned around, and two minutes later we drove up a steep slope into an underground shelter. My friend stopped the vehicle, jumped out and closed the entrance to our shelter with a manually lowered hatch.

"And we're safe."

I looked around hesitantly, but there was nothing to worry about. The dugout was built solidly, stamped and lined from the inside with thin slats. Cabinets and wide benches stood against the walls, while an 'eternal lamp' with a self-charging battery hung from the ceiling.

"It's actually quite convenient here," I remarked, letting go of Firefly, who jumped out of the car, shook himself off puffing out his dorsal comb and began to happily fawn on his master."

"This place was designed to be convenient," Esteban scratched the harpoid on the back of his head. "Enough that you can wait out the storm in peace."

"Peace? When it's howling so loud out there?" I shuddered. The sounds outside really sounded like a horror movie, and even worse, they also had something terrifyingly human in them. The name *living storm* was indeed quite adequate.

Esteban hugged me reassuringly. I snuggled up to him, listening to these nightmarish sounds and involuntarily trying to find whole, understandable words in them. Sometimes I could swear that I really did hear them. Focused on listening to them, I didn't notice what my companion was trying to do, and didn't realize it until he started kissing me. Surprised, I pushed him away reflexively.

"You don't want to?" he was clearly surprised and even a little offended. No, maybe not offended – rather embarrassed.

"No, not like that... I've never..." I stuttered, trying to find the right words.

At first, he didn't understand. Then he turned pale.

"Are you saying that...? How insanely reckless! You could get seriously ill, did the doctor not tell you?"

That's the problem. The doctors prescribed me a variety of medications, including those that kept my hormones at levels that would prevent sexual arousal. They preferred to avoid 'accidental reproduction'? Something like that, I suppose. Apparently, they thought I was such a dumb creature that they didn't expect me to be able to use my gray cells if I fell in love. They probably thought that I would be guided by blind instincts, like an animal. When they stopped giving them to me, I began to feel periods of bad moods, my way of thinking and reactions changed. But still, sexual experiences were not available to me. I knew what they were and what to expect from them thanks to books, films and science programs. However, I did not want to have personal experience in this area. I was ashamed or scared, it's hard to say, at the very least, I could not imagine myself... 'in such a situation'.

"If a person does not engage in regular sexual intercourse, when, according to the Wichmann scale, they are physically and mentally mature enough, they begin to build up stress, which ultimately leads to psychotic behavior. And over time, it becomes more and more difficult for them to establish normal, healthy sexual relations with another person," I remembered an excerpt from a school textbook. Strange, but somehow, I never applied these rules to myself. As if I really live outside the boundaries of not only society, but all human norms.

"Don't be mad," I whispered.

"Of course not," he hastily assured me. "It's not your fault, after all. I won't pressure you, but please go to the doctor and tell them about it all. You may need treatment, but you don't know that you do. Everything will be fine, you'll see."

He spoke to me like to a child, but I hardly listened. I was not at all sure that a visit to the doctor would do anything. Not in my age. I was at the point where I had to deal with everything myself, with the fears and inhibitions that had grown in me. Another problem I ran into.

Meanwhile, Esteban did something else.

"Well, we didn't get to *Little Eden*, but we can still have a picnic. There are canned food and lunch in the lockers, but these are iron rations. We don't need them."

He took a heavy basket out of the trunk and placed it on one of the benches. He covered the low cabinet with a tablecloth he had taken from home and began to lay out everything he had prepared on it: fried cuts of meat, salads in small bowls, salty and sweet biscuits, fruits. Finally, a two-liter thermos.

"Looks appetizing," I admitted.

Because of this cold buffet, the storm howling outside suddenly seemed less threatening to me. Firefly sat at my foot and began to lick his mouth with his split tongue, sniffing impatiently. Esteban tossed him one of the fruits, which looked like a large apple, the harpoid grabbed the treat with his paws and began crunching.

In already a better mood, we sat down to the feast and ate without worrying about the storm. The howls? Let it howl. It can't get into the bunker, and it would obviously stop eventually. And in good company, time flies by. We didn't return to the topic of the failed kiss. In the end, there were so many interesting topics of conversation that we didn't have to focus on what we weren't getting.

*****

Two days after the First Landing Day, Dr. O'Leary decided it was time to awaken Raina. We worked on her together, and in recent days we have been assisted by Roland Marcevaux, industrial chemist, specialist of artificial layer. The doctor insisted that Raina not only returns to full physical capabilities, but also regains her external beauty. As I noticed, the most difficult thing was to find the right color of artificial layer to close the gaps.

"This is because her design is not cataloged," O'Leary explained to me. "It was custom made, like Raul. She is unique."

I could see that myself. There were about ten more androids around the colony, and they all had some kind of, so to speak, template of appearance. The females represented a type of blue-eyed blondes with big breasts, absurdly long legs and narrow waists, while the males looked like animated mannequins from fashion shows – almost the same musculature, an angular playboy face and a trendy hairstyle. Raoul and Raina were different, it was easy to tell that they were *custom made.*

Since it had to take at least twenty-four hours to apply and tie up the artificial skin, O'Leary gave me a break and told me to go home.

"You won't help here and the work will be long and boring," he said. "Go and do some dancing, or whatever you feel like doing."

He knew of my hobby and that in my free time I train hard to stay flexible, using an empty warehouse located on the side of the road, because no one looked in there.

However, this time I decided to do something else. When I ran to work this morning, I stumbled and sprained my leg, which was harmless but rather painful. I had to give it some time to recover. So instead of dancing, I took the easels out of the closet and carried them outside along with a box with all my accessories. I set up the easels, put a sheet of fake paper on the stand, and first, to warm my fingers, sketched from memory the view of the living storm. I worked on it for an hour before finally deciding that it was not half bad. I put the drawing aside and took out a second sheet. I decided to draw a view of the Stone City from the point of view of my garden, as it was now, illuminated by the iridescent sun Jewel.

I quickly sketched in watercolor a general view of the mountain and its surroundings, then washed the image with a sponge to make it clearer. I waited for it to dry and began to work more precisely. I worked diligently, removing from the flat surface the mass of the Stone City with all its details. I was so carried away by painting that I did not even notice how someone entered the garden. It wasn't until he spoke that I flinched and nearly dropped the sharp edging brush I was just working with.

"Well, let the typhoon carry me away..."

Behind me was Terence Vecksler, one of my neighbors, an elderly man with thinning hair and a body that showed a penchant for high-calorie treats. It would have to be quite the typhoon to even lift him off the ground. I heard that he was someone important, but I was not interested in that. We knew each other very vaguely, that is, we said 'good morning' upon meeting and nothing else.

"Good morning," I said hesitantly.

He didn't answer right away. He took the drawing of the living storm, leaning against the leg of the easel, and looked at it carefully. Then he looked at the picture again.

"Can you replicate anything from your imagination?" he asked.

„Yes," I replied in surprise. "With a pencil, charcoal, paint... why?"

He suddenly grabbed my shoulders.

"Girl, you fell down to us from the heavens!"

"In a way, yes, but why…"

"Please leave this for now and come with me, okay?" Vecksler's voice was almost pleading and feverish at the same time.

"Okay, but I don't understand…"

"You will understand everything soon. Please wait for me and don't go anywhere."

He turned on his heel and ran to his home. I shrugged my shoulders and quickly finished the painting. In my opinion, it was okay, but it could be better. I didn't quite succeed in capturing the play of lights on the shining elements and the unusual, interpenetrating colors of the sky over the city. It was very difficult because Jewel gives completely different reflections than the Earth's Sun.

Veksler returned a moment later.

"Come with me please."

"Okay, but where""

"To the conference center. It's not far. I called the whole team."

"What team now?!"

I could hardly keep up with the man who, despite his weight, moved very quickly. I haven't been to the conference center yet; it was almost like a local museum. I had no reason to go there.

Scientists and members of the administration met here, and I was neither the one nor the other. Moreover, I was curious about what I was supposed to do there and what Terence Vecksler wanted from me right now.

The conference room was large and functionally furnished with all the equipment needed for lectures. As soon as I looked around, my guide almost forcefully sat me down on one of the chairs.

"Please wait, miss, everyone will be gathered soon."

"Who?!"

"Planetologists. I'm part of the team."

Another mystery. What could scientists of this class want from me? How was I supposed to help them? After a while they began to arrive – two more men and four women. Everyone was surprised by this sudden call and they were very surprised to see me."

"Terry, what are you doing?" two of them called almost simultaneously.

Vecksler pointed at me.

"Ladies and gentlemen, I present to you the solution to our problems."

"What problems?!" I shouted, feeling that in a moment I will completely lose patience.

"Which problems?" I was echoed by one of the women, a blonde with a tight cut and military jumpsuit. "Because we have enough of them to cover the entire Manhattan Project."

She sat down at the table, propping her elbows on top of it. Her friend, a pretty dark-haired girl in blue pants and a brown blouse, walked over to a primitive machine in the corner and began pouring coffee into mugs. Then she placed them in front of each of us and took out a box of cookies from the closet. Vecksler began to speak, and I was beginning to realize why he was so delighted with my paintings.

The fact that only cable communication is possible on Patris I already knew. Some kind of 'zone' was missing here, I didn't know exactly what. It was natural on Earth, but here it simply didn't exist. Although there was a kind of magnetic field, which, on one hand, did a good job of protecting the planet from external threats, and on the other hand, drowned out short and ultra-short radio waves for almost the whole year, which could have been an alternative. From time to time it weakened for a month or two, and then it was possible to use the radios, although they cracked terribly and the sound was distorted. Other wireless communication was only possible over very short distances, up to half a kilometer. Now I have learned that there was another thing that Patris is preventing its inhabitants from doing.

"We cannot capture the sights," the planetologist said. "The photographs taken with cameras literally melt within a few minutes. We cannot transfer them to paper or any other durable media. Something is interfering with this, and we don't know what. As a result, we cannot illustrate our recordings in any way. We tried everything we could and nothing works. There is probably some type of wave emission that prevents it. Physicists are studying it. Biologists say that whatever it is, it has no effect on living organisms, and they don't care about anything else. While we..."

"The ancient camera obscura seemed to be the salvation," interrupted one of his colleagues. "George Benson, an amateur photographer at your service. It seemed that we could take pictures on film or properly prepared glass, and then transfer them to paper, as was done in the nineteenth and twentieth centuries. The first attempts were rather promising. Then we hit a wall. Patris has no silver, or bromine, which either are not available at all, or there are trace amounts which we are yet to discover. And without silver bromide, we're stuck in place."

I was starting to see the idea. The lack of photographic documentation must have been frustrating, and not just for this team.

"But you could just draw illustrations," I said.

All those present looked at me sadly.

"Well, that's the thing, we can't," said the blonde. "Sydney Morrows, by the way. We examined all the inhabitants of the colony, and none of them can convey the landscape meaningfully. Whoever tried, all we got was some scribbles. We keep them in the documentation, because what else can we do? We don't have anything better yet. You are the first such gifted person we have met here."

Another man, a small gray-haired Asian with an almost boyish face, cleared his throat slightly and decided to introduce himself.

"Gentaro Shimada... late Estrella Solis called it 'the syndrome of no compensation'. In her opinion, by eliminating congenital diseases and disabilities through genetic selection, we also eliminated artists, because artistic giftedness appears as an attempt to compensate for physical or mental disabilities. Time has shown that her theory is correct. The pinnacle of our colonists' capabilities is technical drawing. Of course, there are artists on Earth, but no one would qualify them for such an expedition as ours. Usually they are too emotionally unstable, and even if one of them wanted to come here, they would be eliminated at the first stage of qualification."

I thought it would be better to clarify the situation.

"I would have been, too," I said. "I'm only here thanks to fraud. The Social Commission demanded my elimination under the Disability Law due to inadequate mental level and emotional problems. My dad risked everything to get me into the last group coming to Patris. In fact, I shouldn't even be a full member of your community."

The planetologists exchanged glances, which were, to my surprise, quite amused. They were even smiling, which they tried to hide.

"Miss, there are only three and a half thousand people in our colony right now, not counting, of course, the brats," Veksler said after a moment. "It's as easy to keep a secret here as it is on a department store window. Everyone knows everything about everyone, and each new member of the community is gossiped for good morning."

"We knew about your legal problems from the beginning and we've been observing you closely," Sydney Morrows joined in. It quickly turned out that in this particular case the laws of the Earth are greatly exaggerated, and you are as useful of a member of the community as any of us There is no doubt about that, as we can see now. So, will you join our team as an illustrator?"

I was very flattered by all that, I had to admit it. For many years I thought of myself as a completely useless creature, but then I was hired by a respected artificial intelligence specialist, and now I was given such a proposal... how I regretted that my father couldn't see me now.

"I would love to," I replied. "But what would the doctor say? I think he's happy with my work and I would not want to give up on it either. I like it."

"That's not a problem. You could surely do some drawing in your free time? After all, no one will demand a high tempo or large-scale pictures from you. Currently we are looking for illustrations for our *Compendium of Knowledge about Patris*. Format A4. I guess I can just show you the book..." Gentaro Shimada stood up and opened one of the huge safes lined up against the wall.

They looked like they were planned for a massive explosion, fire, flood and the end of the world at the same time. Judging by the color and visible graininess of the cuts – they were not coated with paint or varnish – they were made from a special alloy. I assumed it was platinum, titanium, tungsten, and possibly something else. Metallurgy was not my specialty, but I could, if my calculations were correct, initially estimate its strength to at least 590 on the *Brinell scale*[2].

Shimada took out an old-fashioned, heavy, leather-bound volume from the inside and handed it to me. The compendium looked rather strange. It was definitely being made by hand, though I guess it couldn't have been made any other way. The individual sheets of paper were framed in an elaborate manner, allowing for more freedom in positioning. Thus, when the knowledge of the subject has been corrected or someone wanted to add something, there was no need to reprint the whole thing. They could then print a corrected or additional page, and pin it in the appropriate spot. Many of them were laminated, so they did not expect any additions here – others were left 'naked'.

"The copy you are holding is the only one in existence. As you can imagine, it is still in the process of being created," Shimada said. "We don't know when it will be finished, if ever. The individual sections are, of course, kept in the form of electronic files and distributed as needed, but this form of the Compendium is our pride. What we want to leave for future generations. Only that without the ability to attach an illustration, there is a lot that is lost. If you could do them, you will not only beautify this book. We can also duplicate them using photocopying techniques and add them to other scientific publications printed on a larger scale. A photocopy is done by spraying a properly prepared powder onto a surface, and it goes through without any major problems. Unfortunately, other methods don't work."

---

[2] Brinell Scale – scale of the hardness of metals and alloys, 1-650.

"Printed?" I repeated. "You print books here, instead of stopping at electronic versions? Why?"

Back on Earth, such distribution still existed for certain works, especially albums, my father had such in the library. However, they were very expensive and inaccessible, even though paper has not been in use for a long time, replaced by synthetics."

"Patris gives us almost everything," Vecksler said. "Among other things, a very common here, fast-growing plant, ideal for the production of strong and resistant to external conditions paper. Without harming the bottom of the natural environment, we have so much of it that we were able to launch a professional printing house that fully satisfied our needs. Contrary to appearances, this is a more environmentally friendly solution than making readers, of which we have too few. Not to mention that they break very easily and we cannot fix them here. As you already know, we are missing several elements, including cobalt. Either it's not here at all, or we just haven't found it yet. As if for balance, Patris is rich in things that are rare on Earth, such as lutetium, vanadium and rhodium. Our research shows that the deposits here are absurdly large compared to ones on Earth. Only that they are relatively of little use to us."

I looked at the unlaminated pages and lightly touched them with my fingers. They were tough, slightly porous. It would have to be primed, but in general, it could be used for painting. Just that...

"Could you copy a larger image and reduce it to a size that fits?" I asked.

"Well, of course. Why?"

"A landscape view looks better on a larger surface," I explained. "Such miniatures are good for reproducing something smaller, a single plant or animal. Or even the geological outline of a mountain. But not a landscape with all its details."

"You will get everything you need," Benson hastily assured me. "We'll make sure of that. Please understand: if something happens, a natural or provoked disaster, an epidemic, whatever it may be... then the Compendium will be all that remains of our work here. That's why we keep it in a safe. It's priceless."

"Each department has its own," added Shimada. "If anything happens here, at least the test results will remain, and maybe someone will read them someday."

I understood them well. I also found this extremely important and felt that I really wanted to be a part of this project.

"I'll do what I can. What should I start with?"

The planetologists looked at each other with obvious satisfaction.

"For starters, could we use the view of Stone City that is currently drying on your easel?" Vecksler asked, "It would be perfect for the inner part of the cover. A kind of graphical introduction to the contents."

"Yes, of course. But let me apply the varnish first, please, since it's watercolor. Then you can copy it however you like. It's better if I use oil paints in the future. Will you deliver them to me?"

"Not a problem," Sydney hastily assured me. "Our technical department will provide any number of paints and chemicals, and I will send a message to the head office that you are on the roster of our team."

Well, well. The exile of society is climbing up. I didn't have a strong sense of sarcasm, but this one spoke to me in a unique way. On Earth, I was less than nothing, here I became almost indispensable for a serious group of scientists studying an alien planet. Hard to believe? And yet. I was eager to tell Dr. O'Leary about this. And, of course, Esteban...

By the way, the old doctor was not at all surprised.

"If you were what the public commission thought you were, I would never have let you into my studio as long as I live," he said simply. "I always thought that IQ tests are something that can be stuffed up you know where. I don't know why they are so trusted. Now, be careful, I'm about to send an impulse to stimulate Raina's cortical centers. Don't approach the alcove until I let you, we don't know how she will act. There were problems with her in the past."

I looked at the android with curiosity, motionless in a device called an alcove, connected to it by hundreds of cables. Raina's smooth chocolate body was no longer damaged, and with her eyes closed, she looked like the Sleeping Beauty in an illustration from one of father's books.

O'Leary pushed a few levers on a large, complex device, which was part of the alcove. The LEDs blinked and a soft hum of transducers was heard. The android blinked furiously, then lifted her eyelids, revealing her beautiful brown eyes.

"Hello, Raina," the doctor said. "How are you feeling?"

"Optimal," she replied in a low, melodic voice. And she added, "The pantry is broken."

"I know. The current shocked you, but everything is fine now. Now allow me, this is my new assistant Aura Maria. She helped me restore your functions."

She looked at me.

"Thank you, miss Aura Maria."

"Remember, she works for me, and you have to obey her."

"Yes, sir."

O'Leary released the clamps, and the cables connected to Raina fell down. Slightly stiff, but in a manner that indicated complete coordination, she stepped out of the alcove and stood barefoot on the littered studio floor. I gave her the dress and shoes that were prepared for her earlier.

"Thank you, miss Aura Maria."

"Aurita is enough," I said without thinking. The android somehow made me feel vaguely caring. There was something helpless and childish about her, something... non-robotic.

She was finishing dressing when Astrid entered the workshop.

"Finally!" she exclaimed joyfully. "I couldn't wait."

Raina reacted oddly to say the least, as she smiled broadly, leapt over to Arstrid and hugged her tenderly like a close friend.

My eyes widened. From what I knew about androids, this was extremely unusual behavior.

"I told you that she is peculiar," O'Realy whispered to me. "She reacts in a way that is hard to predict. She is the most unusual android that I have had to deal with in my whole life. She even beats Raul at that, who is, after all, almost human."

I began to understand his passion for artificial intelligence, a passion devoid of any utilitarianism, even love. Something like that feeling was also awakening in me as I watched Raina greet Astrid and as they both left the workshop, walking towards the house. The happiness that gripped me at that moment was incomparable to anything else.

"You saved a human being, Mac," I said.

He hugged me and kissed me on the top of my head.

"*We* did," he emphasized with fatherly pride. "Come on, kid, we'll start our work on the next project. I have a certain idea that I would finally like to realize."

XI

Ever since they've put me on the list of the planetarians' team, I didn't have much time for myself. And, paradoxically, I had more of it for thinking. Painting is not an activity that engages the mind in any particular way, at least for most of the time. Perpetuating what I was asked to do for prosperity, at the same time I thought and came up with various topics in my head. I already knew that my father had deceived me, although he did it in good faith. He didn't want me to suffer, but he knew he would not be able to join me on Patris. Earthly authorities would never allow this to happen after what he did. At first, I didn't acknowledge this fact, but I think that it was in my head from the very beginning. Lonely reflections at the easel helped me cope with the painful awareness of our parting, although I had to admit that I cried so many times that I had to stop painting and wait for it to pass.

I was glad no one was there to see me. Since the location I was supposed to capture was far from the village, someone from the team drove me here. Esteban will arrive at the appointed time and take me home. That would be our time to talk, joke and even hug a little bit. We haven't mentioned anything since the picnic, neither he nor me. Of course, I didn't go to the doctor, even though I know I should. I postponed this visit from week to week in fear of what I might hear. I had to face the truth – even though I was twenty-one, I was less mature than many sixteen-year-olds, and the thought of sex filled me with fear that I could not yet overcome.

Did I say no one? That wasn't completely true. In the end, Raul accompanied me every time, who was there to make sure that nothing bad happens to me. He began by thoroughly checking the area and surroundings around me and my workplace as a kind of 'electronic shepherd'. He then patrolled the area in search of any and all possible threats, armed with a flare pistol and an alarm gun. This was enough to scare away the local fauna, even those most predatory ones. At my explicit request, the android didn't speak when not asked and did not react to me crying. It allowed me to do what I wanted and feel at ease.

Soon the news of my mastery of brush and pencil spread throughout the colony, and every morning I found a dozen inquiries on my messenger phone, even for modest portraits. I tried to fulfill these orders as much as possible. I started a notebook in which I wrote down the dates so as not to offend anyone. A pencil portrait usually took no more than an hour, including the finishing touches, so the design of the drawing was not difficult. I felt like I was gaining respect through my skills, and it used to be a completely unfamiliar feeling to me. I wish I could share this news with my family, but... that's right.

Diogo and Nando, my father's brothers, still haven't returned from their journey to the icy continent of Patris. All attempts to contact their team have failed. I was wondering why someone would not just fly out there, but I solved this riddle myself, without anyone's help. All I had to do was read. As I noticed, no aircrafts were used at the colony. The only exceptions were the shuttles, which were used to communicate between rockets out of orbit and the landing pad. Its situation was not accidental – it was in this place that a gravitational 'chimney' was formed, preventing the formation of the so-called air holes. On Earth, they got in the way of flying. On Patris they made it literally impossible. That's why the group of glaciologists traveled on hydrofoils, and then on a sleigh with an electric motor. Constant communication during the expedition was impossible, but why were the researchers gone for so long?

"I suppose they can't," doctor O'Leary said, when I mentioned it one time. "They'll be back when they're back. A research expedition to an unknown continent is not the same as a Sunday mushroom-picking trip. Do you have what I asked for?"

I handed him the small portrait, which I painted with oil paints on one of my own pieces of artificial paper. I worked on it during my few free moments, and very urgently. It represented Silver's face, just how I imagined it ever since I was a kid. One time, in a moment of honesty, I confessed to the doctor that there was such a person. And he, to my surprise, took the matter very seriously.

"Draw him for me," he said. "The parts we're working on right now will be used to create a completely new android. I want to train him to be our assistant at the workshop. I didn't think about his appearance yet, but he has to have one. Why not like an Indian? You'll have your dream brother."

"And… you don't think there's something wrong in my head?" I wanted to make sure.

"Of course not. On the contrary, you have it up there better than many that I've known and who I could name. And I know a lot about this stuff. As an andropologist, I first had to finish my psychology degree, before I could start building artificial brains."

The 'doctor of androids' was truly an amazing person, and my opinion of him was constantly improving. I could understand why Astrid, who was about thirty years younger than him, agreed to become his wife and why she loved him so much. I secretly suspected that she loves him more like a father, but the fact remained that she did. And I, too, loved him more and more. In his company, I felt safe and comfortable, and our work together brought us closer. And there was a lot of it, because in addition to the assistant he was going to create, we were also realizing a special order – an android to accompany one of the colonists. I didn't know who it was, because such things were a professional secret, and I wasn't interested in that either. The work itself completely absorbed me.

One could ask how I could find even a few free moments, when every day I fulfilled my duties of the doctor's assistant, and then spent a few hours painting. Well, there weren't many of them, but I didn't really need something like free time all to myself. Even on the contrary, because doing something specific I felt a lot better than searching for entertainment on my own. Once I finished illustrating what was currently asked of me, there was some time remaining, so I took out my own material and painted whatever fascinated me most on Patris. Wonderful clouds, the play of colors in the sky, saturated colors, and the amazing shapes of the vegetation. Sometimes I was able to see some creature in flight, quickly sketch it and finish the picture slowly, taking care of the details. I planned to give these paintings to the biologists later, they really needed illustrations right now.

The *first fall* was just beginning on Patris. As I learned, there were two of them – the *first* was characterized by beautiful, but not too warm weather and usually lasted about two months. Then came the *second* – a month of storms, after which the temperature dropped, which marked the beginning of Patris's winter. On our continent, this didn't mean severe frosts. There was almost no snow, it was only very cold, and the plants enter a state of vegetation. Almost all the animals hibernate. Reptiles dominate Patris, so this is a natural phenomenon for the ectothermic. However, for people, the chills were not particularly acute, and life, as I was assured, went on at that time in a normal rhythm.

The *first fall* had a special meaning to the colonists. It was then that the autumn chess games began, in which Jamie took part. At first, I thought they were talking about traditional chess, but I learned that it was a completely new, locally invented sport. The season of games began with the preparation of a chessboard on a flat area, transformed into a kind of amphitheater. Each square was meter by meter, and the players acted as live chess pieces. They communicated through miniature headphones and laryngophones – for such a small distance, wireless connection still worked. There were ten teams – practically all teenagers belonged to one of them, even if only as reserve players. The winners became something like local celebrities, gaining respect and popularity.

The stands surrounding the board were packed to the last seat. Vendors of drinks and snacks walked around the spectators, a huge board glowed on a tall scaffolding. There were even two cheerleader teams, each consisting of seven girls in brightly colored shorts and decorative tops. As I was told, they were too young to be players, but in the future will apply for admission to the team. For now, they only encouraged the athletes. With traditional pom-poms in hand, they displayed original gymnastic patterns and shouted enthusiastic slogans in support of the teams. Their names could be seen on the scoreboard anyway, with huge letters – Heroes and Conquerors. Jamie played for the Conquerors, who drew white this year. Strictly speaking, it looked like the Earth's Olympics, there was only one fundamental difference.

I knew that a long time ago there was a thing called competitive sports in which real people took part, not machines guided by the minds of their operators, as today, and I subconsciously expected something like that here. But no, the players were only young people dressed in costumes symbolizing the appearance of chess pieces. Of course, the costumes were designed and sewn in a way that doesn't restrict the players' movements. I learned how important this is right after the start of the competition. Jamie, from what I knew, was a pawn in this game. She was dressed in an appropriate costume – a white knit with a short skirt, ruffles around the neck, and a tight hat tied under the chin, with a pointy top, ended with an oblate ball. The girl's hair, sliding from under the canvas, fell in golden-brown waves on her slender shoulders, and her face, framed by a white binder, was shining with joy. My cousin loved these tournaments.

As a privileged person – the player's family – I had one of the best seats, while next to me sat Esteban, who promised me to explain the rules of the game. As he reasoned correctly, I didn't know anything about them, although he still thought I would at least know the rules of the classical chess game. This wasn't the case. Chess was a mystery to me, I could never understand why one time moving forward is good and the other wrong, and why some pieces can move backward or diagonally, while others cannot. I was hoping this wouldn't stop me from enjoying the game.

When the cheerleaders finished their performances, the Master of Ceremony appeared in the tower under the scoreboard, holding a huge megaphone.

"Ladies and gentlemen, it's time to begin the first game of the fall season!" he exclaimed. "As always, the first move goes to the white team! This year, the white team are the Conquerors, led by David Sabatini! Applause to the white team! The Black Team, Heroes, are led by Aelita Sommo, let's hear it for the black team!"

Applause rang out in the stands. A short melody played, probably a hymn, and the white pawn jumped onto one of the empty squares. Immediately after that, the black pawn made a similar move. And a little later I realized what was so amazing about this game."

My knowledge of chess was rather basic, as I've established already. However, like everyone else, I had a general idea, and I knew for sure that in the traditional game, the pieces didn't fight with each other. Here, however, the situation was quite different. When one of the players wanted to take a piece from the opposing team, they had to not only jump onto its space, but also push the opponent out of their zone. Otherwise, they would lose their own space instead, and would be considered out of the game. The rules of the wrestles were not uniform and depended on who fought with whom."

As I found out (Esteban quickly forgot that he was supposed to explain to me what was happening, consumed by cheering), in theory, the pawns had the hardest job as they were not allowed to fight higher ranked pieces upright or use their hands. However, this was only an apparent hindrance, as the players developed a strategy that allowed them to hit the opponent's legs with their whole body like a bowling ball. In general, the higher ranked pieces had more rights, they could, for example, not only grab the opponent, but also strike, though the lesser piece could demonstrate dexterity and cunningness, and still obtain the win. Only equals fought in an ordinary wrestling match, reminiscent of a cross between classic wrestling and old Japanese sumo. Now I understood what Jamie was training at the chess camp. These competitions required not only intelligence, but also good physical fitness.

The Master of Ceremony was not just an announcer. As I noticed, he made sure that the players did not break the rules, and shouted out terms that meant nothing to me, but clearly aroused the enthusiasm of the public. Alekhine's Defense, Queen's Gambit, Gianutio's Countergambit – all this was even more confusing to me than the terminology of analytical geometry, which I could never deal with. So I focused on watching Jamie's fights, glancing from time to time at the scoreboard, where the assistant of the Master of Ceremony changed entries on the board with dexterity, which indicated a lot of training. I didn't know much about the scoring rules, but as I knew White was leading from the very beginning. Finally, I allowed myself to be carried away by the mood of the moment and together with others passionately shouted: "Let's go, Conquerors! Let's go, Conquerors!" and so on. Despite my ignorance of chess, the entertainment really was first class.

The entire colony lived with the tournament for the next two weeks. I was less involved than others and only appeared in the stands when the Conquerors were involved, but most of the fans spent their days there until the finals. The Conquerors took second place, while we're at it. This time the tournament was won by the Daring Warriors team, for which they paid four to one at betting venues. Yes, a type of sweepstake was in function here, it was very popular, although according to the law issued by Governor Eva Svensson right after the elections, the pool of winnings was very limited. Nobody wanted gambling to develop here, but even small winnings made people very happy. They bet not only on the chess matches, as I learned, but also on many other occasions.

The wages were calculated as wages and prices in stores, that is, in diakses, as the local currency was called. Due to difficulties with the introduction of electronic banking, it was decided to use a traditional monetary system from the beginning of the colony. As soon as the first mint was launched, they began paying people salaries in small discs of various denominations. This was very inconvenient compared to the earthly rationing system, but for now necessary.

The diakses were made out of gold, which was in abundance on Patris, as if to compensate for the lack of other precious metals.

Many nuggets could be found in the mountain streams, and in the first exploration quarry they immediately discovered such an abundance that on Earth it would immediately be surrounded by a double cordon of troops, barbed wire and firing squads. There was no such need here. Gold itself in the colony was of little value, more important were clean water and food, the reserves of which had to be taken care of. Precious metals here were only as valuable as was their usefulness in the industry.

The widespread distraction caused by the fall games didn't affect only a few dozen people, including Dr. O'Leary and Eva Svensson. I met her several times while wandering around the empty areas, and I got the impression that she likes this momentary emptiness around her. She smiled at my shy greeting and said:

"You didn't succumb to the sports mania either?"

"I don't know much about chess and I don't like watching people fight," I answered honestly. "Even when it's just a movie, I avoid violent scenes. They scare me. I'm stupid, don't you think?"

"Not at all," she replied politely. "You're simply delicate. That is rare nowadays. But so are artist, and you are, after all, an artist."

We walked side by side for a while.

"Have you received any message from Earth lately?" I finally asked after gathering the courage.

She nodded and looked gloomier.

"I'm preparing for an official announcement. It's not good. The authorities of our home planet have decided to suspend regular flights to Patris. They are very worried."

"Why?" I was scared. "Could it be about me..."

She laughed despite her concern.

"Of course, not... I managed to convince the control on earth that they are dealing with a double deception. Simply put, you weren't in the hibernation capsule at all. That you somehow escaped through the back door and stayed on Earth. They are searching for you now, but they are unlikely to find you, don't you think?"

I should have felt relieved, but the Earth was too far away for me to care what they were thinking.

"Do you have any news about my father and uncle?" I asked quietly.

She looked at me sympathetically.

"Unfortunately, no. I would have to ask directly, and that would raise suspicion. You know what? I will tell my *mole* to dig out some information about them, but it will take time."

"That's okay. I'm still grateful to you. But why were the flights suspended?"

Eva Svensson tightened her lips.

"It concerns the fact that we don't adhere to the rules that we were supposed to not break. Applied genetics is at the core of our social fabric, and we operate contrary to its basic principles. They have the right to be concerned."

I stopped.

"Why is that so important now?" I blurted out in one breath. "Overpopulation has not been a threat to Earth for a long time, let alone here."

The governor looked at me again, but this time in a way as if she didn't see me at all. Suddenly she seemed much older than before.

"It's not that simple. As a society, we are completely soaked with Malthusian ideas. We had to come all the way to Patris before we finally started thinking about the meaning of blindly following the dictates of the eugenic code. The government simply cannot understand that here, we... we simply cannot afford to waste human material. Most of the children on Patris came here from Earth. Very few of them are born in the colony, so we celebrate every birth like the landing of aliens. It doesn't matter if it doesn't meet the standards of a world that struggles with overpopulation, environmental disaster and food shortages."

It seemed reasonable even to me. So why...?

"I know!" I suddenly realized. "The authorities are considering a mass migration to Patris! That's why they want to keep the same rules here as on Earth."

Eva Svensson patted me on the shoulder.

"See, you're not stupid at all. How many people like you have been sentenced to confinement or even euthanasia for failing to learn to solve math tests? But we had to get here and build a new world from scratch before we started thinking for ourselves. We won't give this up, as long as we have a say in it. Patris is our home now. Ours, not the governments of the globalized Earth, which is located in a luxurious fortress somewhere on the Central Island, so God knows where, and considers itself the Council of the Sages."

It all sounded very nice and uplifting, but I had my doubts.

"And what if they try to force us to obey?"

"They can't. The journey to Patris is far too long for them to keep the dispatch of an armed battleship here a secret, let alone a platoon. And our defense is strong, and they know it. And either way, what good an eventual massacre is for them? How will that help them? Things like that only work in epic movies and novels. All they can do is suspend deliveries, which they just did. We'll survive without them. It's worse that we won't get any new blood... but I trust our biologists. They are looking for a way to increase fertility and they will definitely find it. We can do without the help and intervention of the government."

I certainly liked her attitude. Although there was one more thing.

"What are you going to do with the soldiers, since the flights are suspected?"

She shrugged.

"Nothing. We'll wake them up, pack them all into *Armstrong*, and tell them to go home. I've already talked to the pilots and the ship's doctor. They will take command and will not obey anyone's orders until they return to Earth. My men have already searched the ship and confiscated all the weapons just in case. We cannot let them stay, though I'm sure they would rather do so than stand in front of their leadership."

I'm sure they would. They have failed an important mission, so all the anger of the ground control will probably fall on their heads.

"What if there is a saboteur among the colonists they were escorting? Or several?"

The Governor frowned reluctantly, and from the look on her face I could tell that this possibility had also crossed her mind.

"We will take this risk. You can't predict everything, but if you remain alert, you can react in time."

"Are you alert, Your Excellency?"

"Always. My position demands it. I have to remain alert as if a horde of predators awaits me... although, to be honest, I don't know who in their right mind would want such a job. Everything lies on my shoulders, contrary to appearance, even those damn tournaments that I don't care about at all."

I smiled. It was hard not to like Eva Svensson. It's not surprising that the colony gave her so much sympathy and support, although, as I recently learned, there was a group of opposing activists. They believed that colonel Sherman La Ver would be better for the governorship and that the entire colony should be ruled by the military, not civilians. Fortunately, there weren't many of them, and they probably didn't intend to make any actions.

"Did you find out anything about my father?" I asked after a while.

She shook her head sadly

"My contact hadn't found anything. I mean, not yet. Stay optimistic, he will succeed eventually."

I pretended to believe her. Either way, what other did I have? I could not receive messages from Earth myself. Whatever spies the governor had, I'm sure they are skillful. I just had to wait and believe that my father and uncle got through the trouble.

"What are your plans for the weekend?" Svensson asked, looking at discreetly at her old-fashioned watch. She was always in a hurry.

"Mr. Vecksler is going to take me to the sea," I replied. "He wants to see the views there."

The governor suddenly became serious. She hesitated for a moment, as if wondering if she should say something. A whole series of feelings clearly ran over her kind round face. She opened her mouth, then closed it and finally said:

"Be careful."

"Why?"

"I'm sure Vecksler will explain everything to you, this is a topic for a longer conversation. I don't have time for that right now. In any case, please don't come closer than five meters to the water. No matter what happens."

XII

The Patrisian sea looked completely different than I expected. Most noticeably, it was a blue-green color with the transparency of a crystal, so it was easy to see the clumps of coral looming in the depths and various forms floating below the surface. But other than that, it was unspeakably calm, as if tons of oil were spilled on it. Even the smallest wave didn't deform its surface. Which did not mean that it was uniform, because it was not. There were three towers protruding from it in the distance, a little away from the coast. They piqued my interest, I assumed they were observatories built by a team of hydrobiologists.

"Do you like it? I'm sure you were expecting waves, but there's none of that here," Terence Vecksler said. "When the wind blows, then, of course, waves form, and during hurricanes there are some quite big storms. Today it's calm, so the sea is calm like a lake. There is no ebb and flow here. The seas on Earth are driven by the moon, and Patris has no moons. That's why the sea and beach are different."

This was indeed the case. Instead of sand, it was covered in silica plates, smooth as polished mirrors and only slightly covered in dust and debris. Thin cracks were at times visible, but nothing else disturbed this surreal spectacle. I've never been to the beach back on Earth, but I saw it on TV and the difference was astonishing. Only the salty, moist, refreshing smell was probably the same as on our planet many centuries ago. Today the seas of the Earth smell of death, not life.

"When a strong wind blows, everything is blown away, and then the whole beach shines," continued the planetologist. "A beautiful view, isn't it? Something glazed the sand over a large area, and it remained that way. Geologists are still debating whether this is the result of a super strong thunderstorm or volcanic activity. There's one thing we know for sure: sea once covered this area, and it retreated as a result of the area's slow rise. This is why the plates are so smooth. Water has polished them for millennia. But that's not the point now. Look around and tell me what you think is worth capturing."

I looked around as he told me to. The surface of the beach was in some areas indented with hills that looked like sand dunes, but were made of stones as smooth as slabs. All together it reminded me of... a giant stage where sea nymphs could dance. Only in the distance could you see the trees merging into the forests, partly descending to the sea. Mangroves like on Earth. The line of the horizon, merging with the water surface in the distance, glowed with green light, untouched by the fog.

"Should I paint these towers, too?" I asked.

Vecksler cleared his throat in embarrassment.

"Most of all them. Now listen to me very carefully. Please don't go near the water. Stay away from it. Do you see this bright orange line? That is the safe distance."

"I can swim," I assured him.

"Like all of us. It's not the water itself that is dangerous here."

I was genuinely intrigued. I didn't take my eyes off the planetologist, carefully absorbing his words.

"Initially, we were exploring the sea, fascinated by the rich life hidden in its waters," he continued. "Nothing disturbed us in doing so. One day, our nets caught a strange creature, strange even for this planet. It got entangled in the rope and, unfortunately, it strangled him. We took the body to a lab, where our lead xenobiologist Bruno Campbell began examining it. And he discovered something astonishing. Without a doubt, this creature was intelligent. This was indicated not only by its cerebral contents, but also by the fact that it was wearing artificial clothing, which we initially took for some kind of natural formation of the epidermis. Campbell performed an autopsy, then stitched the creature back together, and we agreed to return it to the sea. We figured that the others would certainly start looking for it. Unfortunately, they turned out to be much more rational than we thought."

"What do you mean?" I was confused.

"In the past, underdeveloped tribes often mistook visitors from other places as gods, which made things easier. They... Campbell called them Yogs... had no intention of treating us that way. They are not only smart, but also well developed."

He looked at the three stationary towers and shuddered lightly.

"As psychologist Jensen later said, handing them the body of one of their own could have been taken as a hostile demonstration, and we as the aggressors. Another exploration vessel was attacked and sunk. We've lost several scientists and crew members. Then these structures appeared. They are probably made of coral, but their domes are made of a transparent material, I don't know what exactly," he pulled out military binoculars from under the seat of the car. "Either way, just have a look."

I hesitantly raised the binoculars to my eyes and adjusted the strength of the lenses with a slight flick of my finger. Something was moving inside the transparent dome above one of the towers. Something that looked like... a shapeless lump of sand-green mud, stretching thin tentacles in different directions. I adjusted the zoom to the maximum and I was able to see that this block is covered with some kind of tough material with a green-brown pattern.

"They're ugly," I muttered, dropping my hand. "Why are they called Yogs?"

"Campbell loves old horror books. Those from before the ecological disaster, when people loved being afraid and had nothing to be afraid of. He especially values a certain Lovecraft, hence the name[3].

"In any case, you made the first contact."

---

[3] Yog-Sothoth – a fictional being from the world created by H.P. Lovecraft. It is one of the Outer Gods.

The planetologist snorted with bitter sarcasm.

"First contact, indeed... I guess you could call it that. They lost one member, and due to a accident, and we lost almost twenty. There were even those who demanded a punitive expedition, but fortunately, Sasha Krasusky, who at that time was still in charge, managed to calm down these enthusiasms. There is no point in escalating violence."

I stepped back just in case, although I doubt, they could get me where I was standing.

"What if they attack us?"

"They won't manage. They are not dipnoan. Outside the aquatic environment, they can only last for a few moments. Sometimes, you know, they pop out of these towers if we get too close and make gestures, but they always hide in the domes after three to four minutes. That's the most they can do."

I was relieved, I had to admit.

"Have they not invented something like reverse scuba diving?" I was making sure.

"It's not possible," said Wexle. "Air is compressible, you see, so you can compress it and stuff it into a cylinder. It won't work with water. Their domes are all they can do. They must have a water intake and drainage system so that the guards can breathe freely, but it would have to be difficult to move them around on solid ground. Initially, we were afraid that they would try to fire at us from these positions, but so far there has been no such incident.

We don't even know if they have any weapons capable of launching projectiles far enough to harm us."

We sat side by side on the hood of the car for a while and reflected on it all. Roul, still in the back seat, said nothing at all. We almost forgot about his company.

"And you haven't tried to communicate with them somehow?" I finally asked.

"How? Even if we had a universal translator, there is no underlying database. Besides, the point is not only in the language which we would use to speak with them, but above all in the absence of common concepts and points of reference. Think how many misfortunes have happened in the past, for example, due to the fact that when two civilizations met, certain gestures were understood differently... ah, I guess you don't know history. It's not in the main teaching program nowadays. Etta Solis would understand what I'm talking about."

I squeezed his hand sympathetically, clearly hearing the sadness in his voice.

"We miss her," he sighed, seeing my gaze.

"I didn't know my aunt, but I wish she was still here," I admitted. "She must have been an incredible person."

"No. She was quite ordinary, even at first glance, colorless and silent. But she had tremendous intuition and a wonderful knowledge of society," he forced himself to smile. "People are hardly ever perfect. Practically never. Well, will you paint a few views from here?"

"Of course."

"I'm glad. They are extremely important to the Compendium. Please don't be afraid of the Yogs, they will never attack as long as we stick to the land. We don't know if they have some sort of ranged weaponry, but even if they do, they have never used them against us before."

I should have been scared. I'm sure I would have been if I was the old me. But right now, I was simply curious. I tried to imagine what these strange creatures think about people. They thought we were invaders from whom you need to defend your home, that's for sure. But other than that, how did they perceive us? To us, they looked disgusting, but what about their view of us?"

"Raul will be observing them," I said. "If anything happens, we will hide behind one of these stone dunes and wait."

"Esteban Ponce will meet you at sunset. Just in case, I'll leave a foldable electro board with you, as usual. It makes for a good emergency exit… not that I'm expecting trouble. You are further from the estate than before, but Raul knows the way well and the battery should last long enough."

When I painted, they always left me an electro board. As well as a basket of supplies, which could last me the entire day. The local scientists were very cautious and proactive, it may even seem overblown. However, I understood their distrust of this planet. Previously, they were fascinated and more reckless, which led to the death of many people, so now they behaved as if they were walking through a minefield. They didn't trust even the sites that were checked a hundred times. They also realized that one of them should accompany during my work, but no one had the time to sit back for hours watching me wave my brushes. Fortunately, in their opinion, Raul was enough for my protection, and I agreed with that sentiment.

First of all, I decided to paint the view of the beach. It fascinated me. These regular-shaped plates looked like the result of someone's deliberate actions, and it was hard to believe that this was the work of nature itself. Their smoothness and almost perfect alignment made me want to put on my ballet shoes and perform any dance... for example, the part of the Sugar Fairy from The Nutcracker and the Mouse King... Or Anitra's dance from In the Hall of the Mountain King. I loved this simple, but very fun motive. I had little time for practice now, but my legs missed such endeavors.

In the meantime, I concentrated on the landscape ordered by the planetologists. I painted in focus until the lighting began changing to be more unfavorable. Then I looked up from the easel and saw that on the dome of one of the towers, at the very top, a small hatch had opened. The Yog acting as watchman there stuck out something that seemed to be its head, and then seemed to be trying to figure out what I was doing. It must have looked very interesting, since it decided to stick out to a hostile environment for a short time. I could swear that I also saw a tube, held by its tentacle next to... an eye? In any case, the creature was clearly holding something and pointing at me.

Someone smarter than me probably would have taken into account that this object could have been some kind of weapon and would immediately hide, but for me it was irresistibly associated with an ordinary telescope. At that moment, I didn't think about the possible danger. Perhaps I subconsciously came to the conclusion that if it wanted to shoot me, it would have had enough time to do so. However, I was not as scared as I should have been. Instead, I turned the easel 180 degrees, pointing the painted landscape towards the sea.

The creature first stepped back into the dome, maybe to catch its breath, then leaned out, as if about to fall. The tube in its tentacle lengthened like a telescope. The Yog was clearly looking at what I drew! Without hesitation, I raised my hand and gave it a friendly wave. Well, I thought it was friendly, that is. It's hard to guess what the underwater creature thinks about it, but either way it stepped back abruptly and closed the dome hatch behind it. It didn't show up again that day.

*****

They really liked the beach landscape, and the two additional ones, depicting the 'dunes' and a view of the mangrove forest, even more. In addition to the planetologists, geologists and biologists came to the conference room, who immediately lined up to me – they needed good drawings of the local fauna and flora. The uncritical admiration of my paintings (and you have to believe me, these were not masterpieces) gave me enough courage to ask them about Yogs. Bruno Campbell, a plump brunette, with an almost child-like face despite his rather serious age, immediately started talking. It was clear that the Yogs were like his personal pony, and that he was almost as passionate about them O'Leary was about androids.

"Treating these creatures like barbarians, who kill only for the sake of killing, is a big mistake," he said, hastily preparing a primitive projector. He pulled a flat cassette from the biologists' safe into it. "If an alien race killed, cut up and then stitched back up one of our team members, and then dumped his body to us, what would we think? To them, we are monsters who came out of nowhere and killed perhaps a very valuable member of their community for no reason. No wonder they protect the sea from us. Their behavior clearly states: Live where you want to live, but away from us and the water. Yogs are advanced enough to be able to create some offensive weaponry and shoot it towards us, at least to try to get to those who take samples on the seashore. We did extensive research there and they didn't even try to interrupt us. They only reacted when we broke the waterline. We don't know how to communicate with them, but this behavior should be unambiguous, don't you agree?"

"How do you know they are technically advanced?" I asked as soon as I could get in a word. "Just from those towers that they watch us from?"

"Not just form that, although the very fact of putting up such watchtowers speaks volumes. For example, that they constitute a cooperative society. That they have an understanding of the laws of physics, architecture and biology and some kind of connection... maybe pheromone or vibrative. However, we realized it because of one more thing."

He started up the projector. A film began to scroll across the screen, with a lot of static, full of distortion, but still legible. It depicted a world deep under water, strange and beautiful at the same time.

"Water is partially blocking the factor that prevents us from making a visual recording," Campbell continued. "Unfortunately, only partly. Nonetheless, the information gained from our fish-like probes is invaluable. Fortunately, the Yogs have not recognized them thus far. Every now and then one of them swims to the shore at night and crawls deep into the land for a little while. We know how we programmed them, so we also know where to look. This is one of the many recordings we've obtained. We've received a lot of information from analyzing them... we also have a lot thanks to that unfortunate autopsy."

He changed the cassette to another one.

"What we see here is a type of city built on the seabed. You can see Algae in the distance. The regularity of these fields rather eliminates the possibility of natural formation. The other buildings are likely production halls, but we have not been able to get a closer view so far. We don't want to alarm them, so the sensors work very quietly. However, we've learned quite a lot already, including their social structure. Yogs don't like being alone. They live with at least three people, and often ten, in one large house. Literally none of them live alone. Unfortunately, we don't understand their daily activities, we don't know what is work for them, and what is entertainment, except for the obvious. However, there is no doubt that they are incredibly well organized and use advanced tools."

This was very interesting, and I listened with attention. However, I had other questions that were no less important.

"What about their physical structure?"

Campbell nodded and pulled up an awkward sketch on the screen.

"Yogs breathe through their gills, and have a distinct brain structure and nervous system, roughly resembling what we know from Earth. They have no eyelids, like most aquatic creatures, and their eyes, about four protruding around the head, are about the same as those of Earth's octopuses. It's hard to say if they hear the way we hear, but they can definitely sense vibrations. Their internal structure is also similar to the standard, although not entirely classical – a circulatory system with a double heart, gills resembling an organ similar to the Earth's axolotl."

I tried to remember that creature with some difficulty. It was like a kind of lizard with feathery outgrowths on both sides of its head.

"The digestive system consists of several small stomachs, a kind of highly developed liver, and four endocrine glands, the functions of which we do not understand," the biologist continued. "Of course, there's also the intestines and the excretory system. The most interesting thing of all, though, is their musculoskeletal system and the skin layers. In fact, one is indistinguishable from the other. These tentacles are not constants, so to speak. They are more like fake legs, like those of amoebas. Yogs push or squeeze them as needed. Therefore, their clothes have a very peculiar cut so as not to interfere with the usefulness of such a body design. They also have organelles that they use to generate electricity, just like Earth's electric eels. Perhaps by connecting individuals in a group, they can achieve very high voltages. Those of ours who fell into the water during the attack on our ship died precisely from an electric shock."

"We must look really weird to them," I remarked. "How do they communicate?"

"We have no idea," he admitted honestly. "They have no voice apparatus as far as we can tell. Their mouths are located on the underside of their body, and they are unlikely to use it to talk. We suspect that they use vibrations and pheromones, but they can likely also hear, and almost certainly some of their communication is done via some kind of dance, similar to the dance of Earth's bees. We were able to capture what you could call that several times. Would you like to see?"

"Oh, yes!"

It sounded really interesting. Bruno Campbell rummaged through a box with cassettes, and after a few moments fished out the right one. He inserted it into the hole of the projector. An image appeared on the screen, with as much static as the others, but this time with traces of attempts to clear it of annoying distractions. Thanks to them, it became much clearer and, in addition, contained what biologists were interested in – a couple of Yogs, absorbed in what looked like a discussion. They circled around each other, swinging their tentacles, usually once 'danced', while the rest watched, sometimes making some kind of tentacle gesture. Then the second one did the same. Sometimes two of them 'danced' at once, as if shouting at each other, while the rest tried to separate them. The bizarre figures of the Yogs acquired a strange, unreal grace in movement that I would never have suspected of them. Everything looked so rhythmic that I could almost hum a melody to the dance.

Bruno Campbell was clearly happy with my interest.

"At first we thought it was mating behavior," he explained. "After a lot of analysis, however, we concluded that there was nothing pointing to that conclusion. While we still don't know how they reproduce, this is probably not how. The versatility of such dances clearly shows that this is a kind of exchange of experience. Of course, we don't understand any of it... Dr. Salitzky, our cryptologist, is trying to work out individual gestures by analyzing their frequency, but she doesn't have a reference point. And neither do any of us. So far, she has identified only two gestures, and that's still a success."

"Which ones?" I looked at him with wide eyes. How could you single out something repetitive from this chaos of movements without losing your mind?

"First one: two tentacles connected above the inset of the head, it means something like 'good morning', because they repeat this every time they meet. The second, one of the tentacles, lowered vertically down and sharply curved at the end, like the letter V, is goodbye. This is all our knowledge. You have to admit, it's not much."

It was hard not to admit. However, in the end, it was still something. And I'm sure it required hard, systematic work.

"They say hello and goodbye, which means that they have something like a culture of everyday life," I dared to express my thoughts aloud. "They are undoubtedly an intelligent race and possessing the achievements of civilization. Why don't they try to communicate with us somehow? Learn something about us?"

"We don't know. Maybe they are, in their own way, and we just can't register it? And they wonder why we don't answer?" Sydney, who listened to all this with boredom, as she already knew the topic, decided to join the conversation. "However, it is possible that the message addressed to us sounds something like: *Get the hell out of here, now!* They don't have to necessarily be as interested in us as we are in them."

I thought of the Yog watching me paint. It was definitely curious. I was doing what he could not understand. Undoubtedly, the underwater civilization didn't know about painting, because how would one paint underwater? An idea began to crystallize in my mind, which I didn't tell to the scientists. They could have laughed at me or, worse, forbid what I was thinking. And I didn't want that. I just felt that I was right, although I could not defend it in a discussion with someone smarter than me. For the first time in my life, I realized what seemed illogical: the one with the highest IQ in society is not always right. Nay! Even the most educated one. There are situations when instinct is more important, the feeling that something needs to be done this way, and not another way."

I remembered a travel book that I read a long time ago.

"Two points left and then stop!" shouted the captain.

The helmsman obeyed, though he trembled with fear and prayed in silence for the ones dying. The tropical cyclone roared around the fragile ship like a hundred angry beasts. The sailors froze in their places, convinced that in a moment there would be only splinters from the 'Princess of the Seas' and they will only find a graveyard at the bottom. Some wept, others prayed, if they knew how, and others, including me, cursed loudly. Only the captain remained relentlessly calm, suppressing any sign of panic with sharp orders.

The ship, meanwhile, got stuck in place and didn't even sway. Clouds and swirls of water swirled around it, but literally nothing was happening where we stood. In the end, everyone realized that by some unimaginable miracle they had found the 'eye' [4] *of the cyclone – an almost microscopic area where it was possible to survive such a storm and where absolutely nothing happened. And when the storm subsided, they sailed on, passing the wreckage of other less fortunate vessels along the way.*

The 'Princess of the Seas' sailed slowly so that the sailors could spot survivors and bring rescue to those who didn't die in the cataclysm. Right now, it was the priority, and even I, who was not even a sailor, and had a very limited reserve of physical strength, got involved. We picked up a total of twenty-six sailors and nine passengers, holding on to the floating planks of the shipwrecks.

"How did you know what to do, sir?" a senior boatswain dared to ask when we entered the port of Cadiz.

The captain turned to him. His hair visibly grayed during that night, but his eyes remained stony and not a single muscle on his lined face twitched. He looked like the god of the oceans.

"I didn't, Mr. Kimbley," he replied. "I have no idea why I gave such an order."

---

[4] Eye – the center of a tropical cyclone. In a cyclone's eye the weather is calm. There is also no rain in this area, although the temperature is raised, while the pressure is very low (below 960 hPa).

XIII

During this period of time, I stopped thinking of myself as someone useless, stupider than my whole neighborhood. I was still aware of my limitations, but the disadvantages no longer obscured my benefits. I developed something I've never had – self-confidence. Dignity, which I didn't think I had the right to before.

Dr. O'Leary unexpectedly gave me a week off. He needed chemogel to start the new android's brain, and all his supplies were depleted. The production of the new one was supposed to take only seven days, and I wouldn't be of any use there during that time. So, I received a vacation which I could spend how I wanted to. Therefore, on the first day, I decided to realize my plan.

Terence Vecksler was overjoyed to hear that I wanted to spend all day painting, and happily took me and Raul to the sea. He needed a view of the towers and the panorama behind them for the *Compedium*, as well as the arrangement of clouds over the sea, which, when illuminated by the sun, created such unusual spectacles at different times of day that it was difficult to believe they were real. And it was their volatility that I had to capture with a brush.

"If it was possible, I would photograph the clouds here all day," the planetologist admitted. "Maybe we'll find a way some day. For the time being, you are our only chance to consolidate these natural miracles."

Well, there have been no other methods for millennia. Strictly speaking, since the beginning of humanity. Many of my father's books have talked about this and illustrated the text with photographs of the first rock paintings, Greek amphorae, Chinese mosaics and the later brush masters. The photograph didn't appear until the 19th century. Here on Patris, history is in full swing. Only that that there were no masters or even self-taught geniuses, just me, slightly talented amateur with a palette and a box of paints. It was easy to see why Aunt Estrella was so sad about all this. How I wished I had the opportunity to meet her, even though when reading her notes I sometimes felt like I was talking to her. Not that they were of great literary value, because, as far as I could tell, they weren't. However, they contained a lot of interesting thoughts and notes about life.

Painting the layouts of clouds is not easy since they change so fast. All I can do is do it quickly and save the details for later. That's what I did, putting the sketches one by one on the sand to dry them at least a little before putting them in a special set of separators given to me by a team of botanists. When I finally lifted my eyes from the easel and set the brush down to take a short rest, I saw a Yog in the middle tower open the hatch and look outside. I reached for a pair of powerful military binoculars.

It was hard for me to tell with certainly, but in my opinion, I was dealing with the same curious individual as before. After setting the binoculars to maximum magnification, I could even judge the color and texture of its skin. It was a little rough, sand-likes in some places, and different shades of green in others. The rhythmically puffing out feather-like gills covered something, from which a long tube went down and disappeared inside the tower. I guessed it was a breathing apparatus and that thanks to it, the Yog could look at me freely without choking on the air that was deadly for it.

For the first time, I also saw one of its eyes, round, bulging, and black. That's what we put the telescope lens to. I was also interested in what its lenses could be made of, because I'm guessing that the Yogs couldn't work with glass deep underwater. They still came up with a way, though, considering they had such a device. The domes of the towers were also transparent, so this technology had to bc well developed on an industrial scale.

I took the time to call Raul.

"I'm listening, Domina," he looked at me questioningly as he approached.

"Can you throw objects so that they fall far away from you?"

For a moment I felt like he was smiling.

"My range has been measured. I can throw a sports disc over two hundred and fifty-four meters if I throw from a full swing. Other distances depend on the weight and shape of the object."

"Very good," I opened the food basket and pulled a flat package from the bottom, prepared in secret from everyone.

It contained the best painting I could manage of a woman and a man standing on a high cliff holding hands against a starry sky background. Behind them, I placed a view the Earth's globe with marked seas and continents and a model of the ship on which the first expedition arrived. The people were naked, but at their feet were clothes, painted in a way so that they could be looked at. I hesitated for a long time to add a gesture of friendship to my models, but the Yogs could misunderstand, so I opted for neutral poses. Instead, I painted on the edges a precisely simplified diagram of the development of embryos, males and females, from sperm and egg to birth and then – in a simple and abbreviated way – to adulthood. The last stage was the people standing on a cliff.

I secretly laminated the finished picture at night in the conference center, where the relevant machine stood. Then I carefully framed it into a wooden frame so that it would not sink when it was in the water. Now I passed it on to Raul.

"Throw it so that it hits the water as close as possible to the middle tower."

Android took the painting and looked at it. Then he looked at me.

"Are you sure, Domina? Attempts to contact aliens are currently prohibited due to the many deaths."

"Raul, my dear, I don't think they really want to kill us. They more likely want us to stay away from their home because they're afraid of us," I explained. "And I think we are more like the aliens who have raided them. I am sure. Throw it."

Without saying anything else, he turned and flicked his arm wide into the sea. As expected, the Yog jerked and hid in the tower, slamming the hatch behind it. It would probably take a while before he checks what was thrown at it, so I ate something and went back to work. I had enough of it to make time pass quickly.

Nothing else happened that day. Before dusk, Esteban picked me up and took me home. We exchanged a few kisses along the way. I was less tense than before, though kissing still seemed strange and somewhat unhygienic to me. I didn't like it very much and, in the end, I asked Esteban to stop. I must have hurt him, but he tried to hide it as best he could. I didn't understand my reaction myself, after all I liked him more and more. But there must have been something serious stopping me.

The weather was looking grayer starting from the next day. Open-air paintings were out of the question for now, so I started working on improvements and finishing touches, while Raul went to the hospital. I had a lot of time to think and around noon I decided it was time to consult a doctor. It wasn't just because of my conversations with Esteban, but disturbing symptoms. For some time now, when I woke up at night, I felt a strange tension and pulsation in my lower abdomen. I was overwhelmed by the heat, concentrating mainly on my private part. Indeed, it was about time to see a doctor.

The medical center was divided into the main hospital building, where Dr. Linde and Raul worked, as well as several smaller clinics. I already visited one of them, at the very beginning, when I had to undergo a series of tests, but there was no need to again after that. At least that's what I thought. As a result, I didn't know who to go to now. Dr. Linde was out of the question, not only because of our intimacy, but because he was a surgeon. I needed an internist and maybe a good psychologist. The problem was that none of the names on the clinic lists meant anything to me. Esteban would could have probably recommended someone, but I didn't want to let them know about my problems. I didn't dare talk to Tina Roberts because she aroused a vague fear in me. Maybe because she was a local law enforcement officer, and therefore had to be strict and uncompromising.

After a while of picking from the list, I decided to choose doctor Aida Polasky, mostly because, from all the interns, she was the only one who was certainly a woman. I did not want to confide in a man, and there would be no point to my visit if I didn't tell them everything that's bothering me.

The doctor turned out to be an older woman with a pleasant smile and slightly graying hair. As I noticed before, Patris wasn't able to launch a production line of antiage pills, because the age variation in people was much more visible than on Earth. Taking the right medications made it impossible to distinguish a forty-year-old from a sixty or even seventy-year-old there. Here the differences were visible and clear as in the palm of your hand, not only because of the condition of the skin or figures. It was also easy to tell someone's age by their hair. There wasn't anything available against balding here, so they accepted it as well. Plant decoctions were used to dye hairstyles, which were not always 100% effective. Gray hair and baldness – virtually invisible on Earth – were therefore an integral part of appearance in the colony. It seems they were not as concerned with it as one would expect.

Stuttering and blushing, which I could clearly see through the mirror on the wall, I laid out my problem to the doctor. At the same time, I had to start from the very beginning so that she would understand where it came from and why I didn't start normal intercourse when my peers did. Doctor Polasky listened to me carefully, not changing her expression and not interrupting my embarrassing confessions until I was finished. It wasn't until I stopped talking and looked at her expectantly that she sighed heavily.

"I'm sorry to say this, but your father really hurt you."

"That's not true!" I protested vehemently.

"And yet it is. For selfish reasons, he cut you off from society and its rights, using his contacts and money for this purpose. If you were taken as a child to a working-class neighborhood and raised there, you would have grown up among peers who would not treat you like you're insane. That social class doesn't pay attention to IQ, and your extraordinary talents and personal charm would undoubtedly be appreciated there," she rubbed her lips with her finger, visibly reflecting on the choice of words. "Higher classes make a logical error, thinking of technical workers as commoners, and about themselves as aristocracy. Your father is no exception."

She probably thought I was in shock, but she was wrong. Long time ago, I came to similar conclusions, although I didn't want to clearly acknowledge them. I loved my father indiscriminately, and

I wanted to defend him from the whole world should the need arise. Nevertheless, it was hard for me not to honestly admit to myself that the doctor was telling the truth – very unpleasant and inconvenient, but still the truth.

"There's no way to change that anymore, anyway," I said brusquely. "I came to you for a prescription to my problem. What do you want me to do?"

She rubbed her lips again, clearly wondering what to say.

"It's not that simple," she finally admitted. "When a young person is physically and mentally mature enough, they should begin regular intercourse without delay. It is essential for the maintenance of hormonal balance and therefore physical and mental health. In your case, the critical time was exceeded by several years. You had your endocrine system in check with blockers, and when you stopped taking them, everything went crazy. Truth be told, I have not dealt with such a drastic case before."

"Why do you say drastic?" I was scared because the doctor's voice sounded very serious. She was no longer smiling.

"You admitted that you're dating someone you really care about. And yet, you don't want to allow him to get close. Why?"

"I don't know," I admitted honestly. "I think my body wants something else than my mind does. Sometimes I wake up at night feeling horny, colloquially speaking, but at the very thought of letting any man into my bed, even Esteban, I feel some inner resistance. It's so powerful that I can't break through it."

"And yet you're still asking?" Aida Polasky raised her eyebrows slightly." You've developed a mental block that will be difficult to deal with."

"Maybe..." I hesitated. "Maybe I'll just grit my teeth and..."

"No," she interrupted me sharply. "Not under any circumstances. You cannot force it, it can result in trauma that you will be dealing with for the rest of your life. If we want to hope that you will ever have a normal sexual relationship, we must tread carefully. I will prescribe you something to soothe and alleviate your symptoms and I'd like you to come to psychotherapy. Twice a week in the office across from mine. Andrea Mastroiani, a renowned therapist, will take care of you. Don't be afraid of her, she is a great specialist and a very nice person. You will definitely like her."

Maybe she was right and I really needed therapy. I really felt like I needed it anyway. The problem was that I didn't like doctors and I was afraid of them all my life. For good reason – on Earth they literally had power over life and death. But in my family home, I had to hide from official factors and act like I was some mutant. I was in danger. Here, I don't have to hide, and I'm free from the decision-makers, so the reason for the fear disappeared. Even so, it was still difficult to force myself to visit a doctor. And now I would have to visit a therapist... yes, it wasn't easy, but I faced it. I could be proud of myself.

Rudzia greeted me at home, jumped and spun with a cheerful kiss like a normal pet, happy with her mistress's return. One could forget sometimes that she is made of microprocessors. I took her in my arms and stroked her fluffy fur and sat in a chair by the window. Raul had not yet returned from the hospital, where he worked as an outpatient assistant. The rain rattled the windows and covered everything with a gray curtain. There was nothing to do in such weather. Compared to the Earth's network, cable television here had a woefully modest offer. I should have used this time to correct my sketches, but currently I had no motivation for it. The season of bad weather wasn't called the *suicide season* for nothing. Something happened to the aura at this time, something that had a strong effect on people's minds. And although this part of the year lasted only four to five weeks, it made psychiatrists very busy. Now I had the opportunity to see that those who told me about it were not exaggerating.

It was only the first day. After that, it would only get worse rather than better. Life in the colony stopped. People did only what they really needed, and after work they locked themselves in their homes like rats. The youth and children spent this time in the school complex, where they had days full of study and exercise, and spent the night in a boarding school. It was to strengthen social ties and teach cooperation, as well as to prevent frustration and 'stupid thoughts' amongst this group of colonists. The adults had to deal with it as best they could.

As for me, I could deal with this situation better than most, since after all, after years of loneliness and silence, I've gotten used to it. Although after a couple days, I felt like I couldn't take it anymore and had to leave the house for a while. I found an umbrella in the closet Estrela used and started walking to Esteban's house. I tried contacting him several times on the videophone, but only the answering machine answered. It could be a malfunction, or that Esteban didn't want to talk to me. He may have come to the conclusion that he was unnecessarily involved and changed his mind. I wouldn't even blame him, but I wanted to hear it from his own lips instead of having to guess.

The neighborhood was drowning in mood. The stone paths, which could be used to walk without falling up to your knees in the wet ground, were already so muddy that it was difficult to see a relatively safe path. I slid on the wet stone slabs, trying to keep my balance, soaked, until I finally arrived at Esteban's house. The umbrella, though firmly made and bent into a deep dome, did not help much against the penetrating wind and downpour, which didn't subside even for a moment.

No one answered the bell or the knock. I was about to stop and go back home when I heard Firefly's scratching and pleading squeaking. I became worried. The harpoid didn't like being left alone at home, but then happily responded to someone's arrival. Now his voice sounded desperate, as if calling for help. I squeezed the doorknob and the door opened in front of me. Firefly jumped into my arms. He hissed and creaked as if crying, and as I hugged his reptilian body, much lighter than might be expected at this size, I felt it tremble.

I forced myself to go inside. Esteban lay motionless on the bed, his eyes open and fixated on the ceiling. On the bedside table, leaning against a mug, stood a stiff piece of paper with the calligraphic inscription, "I can't do this anymore. Please forgive me." The world started to spin in front of my eyes, and I fainted for the first time in my life.

After about twelve minutes, I regained consciousness. My elbow was in pain, which I hit against the table as I fell, my head ached and Firefly huddled beside me. I had to get it together. A nervous attack in such a situation would not change anything and the relevant services had to be called. I found a videophone, turned it on, and dialed the police station number. The face of a young boy appeared on the small screen, who probably haven't even had the time to shave yet.

"Officer Adam Rand, I'm listening," he said, trying for his voice to sound as 'adult' as possible.

"I'm reporting suicide. Celine Estate, square 12B, plot 184," I didn't know how I managed to speak calmly and to the point in this situation.

"I'm sending a patrol!" the boy jumped out of his seat and I heard as he shouts: "Mrs. Commander! Mrs. Commander! We have another suicide!"

Tina Roberts appeared in the field of view of the camera, visibly nervous. When she looked at the screen, she became even more worried.

"Aura Maria, is that you? How unlucky that something like this must have happened to you. Listen carefully: my people will be there soon. I'll also call the ambulance. Don't move from your place and don't touch anything."

I had no intention to do that. At this point, I finally lost control of my nerves. I sat in the corner and cried bitterly.

The police patrol and the medical team found me this way, hugging Firefly convulsively, with attacks of hysteria. Dr. Polasky, summoned by Tina, first gave me an injection to calm me down, and only after a long time convinced me to go to the ambulance. I didn't want to let go of the harpoid, so she let me take him with me.

"Doctor, is it me... is it because of me...?" I stuttered out when I could finally say something.

"No," she said firmly. "You must not think so. Maybe I shouldn't reveal a medical secret, but Esteban Ponce has been suffering from severe depression since his wife's death. He didn't want to be treated, he believed he could deal with it alone. As you can see, he was wrong."

I shuddered even more.

"If I were kinder to him..."

The doctor put her hands on my shoulders.

"It wouldn't change anything," she said emphatically. He might have been planning it for a long time, or he could have succumbed to the season. It was impossible to predict. I'm afraid that whatever you would've done, you wouldn't have saved him. Depression kills even on Earth, let alone here. Ponce should have had an android for company, but we didn't have one available. O'Leary was going to build one, and I know was even working on it... but he didn't do it in time."

"We ran out of chemogel," I whispered, sniffing. "Her name is Rebecca... She's very pretty. I didn't know she was supposed to be for Esteba... we built her at the same time as another android who was supposed to be a workshop assistant. It was not possible to start the brain without chemogel and its production is difficult and time consuming."

"I don't know much about the construction details. It's too bad you didn't finish her. On the other hand, it's not guaranteed to have helped either, Mr. Ponce's illness was too advanced. Right now, we have to take care of you. We'll take you home and you'll get additional medicine. Please take my words seriously and take them three times a day if you want to protect yourself from such a fate."

Once I was home, I found Raul there. Tina Roberts contacted the hospital and demanded him to be immediately sent home so that I wouldn't be alone. The android, without asking any questions, helped me undress and get to bed. The firefly curled into a tight ball beside my side, trying to take up as little space as possible while still squealing pathetically. Raul lifted a chair, sat down next to the bed, and took my hand protectively. I needed that. Despite the sedatives, I was still shaking.

"You know, Esteban is dead," I whispered.

"I know," he replied calmly. "Mrs. Roberts said that he succeeded this time."

"This time?"

"He has attempted it before. He was very ill, but the treatment seemed to work. The doctors must have been wrong."

His balanced, cultivated voice gave me some relief.

"Why was his condition so bad? Do you know anything about it?"

"Too many bad things have happened to him. He lost his father on Earth, then here his mother and finally his wife. He also greatly experienced the death of Domina Estrella. She was his favorite teacher."

It sounded reasonable. So maybe what happened really wasn't my fault?

"Can that really kill someone?" I tried to make sure and looked up at Raul.

"I don't have enough data," he said after a moment's thought. "But Dr. O'Leary said that suffering is like aspirin to a human being. It serves the heart in small doses and destroys it in large doses. It is likely that this is what happened to Mr Ponce."

Rudzia woke up, stuck her face out of the box on the shelf, and pecked a few times. I reached for her with my free hand. She over it to my shoulder and pressed against my neck. I hugged Firefly.

"You are my family," I whispered to Raul, "you, Rudzia, and this tamed bird-reptile. I don't think I will have anyone else."

"And Domina Gemma? She's the daughter of your father's sister, so you're family."

I shook my head and finally became sleepy.

"I have nothing in common with her. We are strangers to each other, like two distant planets in space."

XIV

After a week of fine-tuning my sketches and swallowing pills, I felt strong enough to go back to work at Dr. O'Leary's lab. I was just in time. The chemogel has finally stabilized, so we could begin advanced work on the androids. As I found out, there was more to it than assembling the memory banks into a complicated network and then immersing them in this unusual preparation. The work was insanely complicated, and O'Leary, of course, did all the manipulation himself. I could only watch, or sometimes serve as an instrumentalist, and that in itself was a great honor.

We both wore wetsuits that resembled the costumes of astronauts working in space or the old sea divers. Before entering the dust-free laboratory through the air chamber, we took – already in full suits – two showers, one blowing and one ozone shower, as well as a two-minute ultraviolet sterilization. And before starting work, O'Leary turned on the technical air conditioning to maximum, so all the air was filtered every two minutes.

"Anything could disrupt the delicate joining of molecules in the chemogel," he explained. "You may not believe me, but this place is ten times cleaner than the operating room."

I didn't know at what scale could you measure the cleanliness of one room compared to another, but I was tempted to believe him. This lab was the apple of the old doctor's eye and he didn't let anyone in. Apart from him, only spider-shaped construction machines worked there, sterilized in all the possible ways known to mankind. Someone unfamiliar with such subtle technology would find it to be obsessive, but I knew the doctor wasn't exaggerating at all. The mess in the workshop did not bother him, he was also rather indifferent about personal hygiene. Yet in some strange way he knew how to combine personal negligence with the strict requirements of a dust-free laboratory.

The work on the nervous system of both androids was therefore in full swing. It was very tiring. Despite Esteban's death, the doctor continued to work on Rebecca.

"She is not a bike," he explained abruptly when I dared to ask. "A baby will continue to grow in the womb of the mother, even if she changes her mind or when the family ceases to exist. Once you begin the work on an android, you must continue building it until it responds on its own and becomes a fully rational being. This is the basis of andropological deontology[5]"

Andropology is the study of androids, just as anthropology studies people. My father was a world-famous anthropologist. Maybe that's why he hated the idea that his beloved only child

---

[5] Deontology – in other words, a collection of rules of professional morals.

would become an ordinary worker. I couldn't stop thinking about it. What would he say now that he found out that I had become an assistant to someone like MacLean O'Leary and was accepted into the planetary science team? He would certainly be proud. I wished I could send him a message. Perhaps it will be possible one day, once the people on Earth understand certain issues. Eva Svensson was still in correspondence with the Earth's authorities, trying to explain to them the specifics of the Patris reality and the reasons why not every law strictly observed on the home planet could apply here. We could only hope that they would understand it one day.

The first day after the rain stopped, I returned to the sea. Since I was not afraid of the Yogs, the planetologists decided to take advantage of all the possibilities that painting in this area offered. The sea fascinated them all the more because they didn't have direct access to it. I guess this could explain why there were no attempts to make contact with the research expedition on the ice continent, tentatively called Winteria. And why they weren't coming back. Ever since the towers emerged, they stopped violating the borders of this reservoir, since they didn't want to provoke the rulers of the seas. The ice researchers had to manage on their own until their work was finished. I knew they would try to come back later, and I hoped the Yogs would let them through or be unable to destroy their hydrofoil. Apparently, it was very well-built, but of course the danger was still there.

This time, it was Gentaro Shimada, a very nice, always smiling Japanese man, drove me to my usual place of work. After promising to return before sunset, he left to do his own matters, and I began setting up my equipment. As always, Raul walked around the premises looking for signs of danger. At one point I heard him call, so I left the stand and walked toward the voice.

"There's something there," he said, pointing to the demarcation line.

Indeed, on the orange stripe lay, showered clean by the rain, lay some object – quite large, white, looking from a distance like a seashell or a large porous stone.

"Bring it to me," I ordered.

What the android handed me was definitely not a shell. I held in my hand an object that looked like an openwork sculpture, made with excellent craftsmanship from something resembling coral. It was not uniformly white, had blue and red accents, and clearly bore traces of machining. I turned it in my hands, trying to understand what it meant, and from time to time looked up at the towers. Today they were quiet and peaceful, nothing moved around inside them.

"Don't tell anyone about this," I told Raul. "I will examine it later."

I hid the find on the bottom of the food basket and went to work. My hands were shaking with excitement, because I had no doubt that I had received an answer to my gift to the Yogs. I didn't know what it was yet, but the fact that it was from them was indisputable. I couldn't wait to get home where I could examine this item in peace.

A careful examination, to my disappointment, didn't help much. The sculpture pleased with its careful processing and precision, but its abstract form was completely incomprehensible to me. Unable to hold back my absorbing curiosity, I went to see Dr. O'Leary in the middle of the night. He usually worked late, so he wasn't yet asleep, but he was surprised to see me.

"What, are you suffering from insomnia? For me, an old man, that's nothing strange, but you?"

I handed him the item and explained how it ended up in my hands. The doctor's pale blue eyes widened in surprise.

"You are crazy, you know that?"

"I know," I admitted regretfully.

He looked intently at the statue from all sides. At first he probably understood as much as I did of it, but then his eyes lit up.

"I think I get it!"

He brought one of his beloved diagnostic devices to the table.

"It's a laser stereoscope compressed with a reader based on a vibration pattern," he explained. "Take a look."

He placed the statue in the diagnostic chamber and turned it on. For a long time, he fine-tuned the parameters, especially the vibration frequency, an extremely difficult thing that I didn't yet know how to do. Ultrasound rays and waves began to sweep the strange object, and after a while an enlarged hologram appeared above the tabletop. I sighed in amazement.

The sculpture turned out to be something completely different than I thought. It was not a work of art, but a technological object.

Proper tuning of the stereoscope revealed a complex, MOVING sight – two Yogs touched each other with their tentacles in a dance, and then placed their tentacles together on the third one, that had appeared from the ground. Then they withdrew. In the foreground appeared a stranger whose side suddenly bulged and released what looked like an elongated egg. The creature moved its tentacles as if digging a hole in the ground, the 'egg' slipping into it and disappearing. The Yog swam aside to his relatives. From the place where the 'egg' had vanished, a thick stalk shot out, as if consisting of overlapping plates. After a while, they parted and each of them began to look like a miniature Yog.

I couldn't find the right words. Dr. O'Leary was more eloquent than I was, so he was the first to speak, though the holographic sight seemed to shake him no less.

"They understood your message. In response, they provided us with a pattern of their own reproduction. And in something," he looked at the reader's chamber, as if enchanted, "something like this. It's so complicated that I lack the technical terms. Like a movie in a pill. These blue and red impurities create a stereoscopic effect and the motion mimics the material's response to vibration."

"How did they know that we would have a suitable reader?"

"They didn't. They decided to take the risk. They figured that we have highly developed technology, so even if we didn't have anything suitable yet, we would be able to build it."

He looked at me with reluctant respect and I felt myself blushing red. I was able to do something that people much smarted than me failed to do – I made First Contact. I should be undoubtedly proud of it, but right now I felt a bit scared.

"What next?" I asked helplessly.

"Next we'll show this gem to our scientists. But not right now, of course. For now, get some sleep. Tomorrow a true bomb will explode here. Be prepared to get thoroughly reprimanded, since the big guys will probably say that you've put the entire colony in danger and blah blah blah."

"Oh no!" I was scared. "Can they get me in trouble?"

"No, of course not, they can only complain. I'll be there with you, so don't worry," he patted me on the back with obvious amusement. "Science is a risk, my dear. Almost no one remembers it nowadays. They will probably take offense to their pride, but pay that no mind. It sometimes happens that a talented dilettante achieves something that hordes of scholars educated up to the nostrils have been trying to in vain. They will have to come to terms with it."

*****

The old doctor's support turned out to be invaluable. Life has taught me neither to fight for my own nor to defend my position in meaningful discussion. When I'm attacked, all I can do is cry, and that's useless in the long run.

The first reaction of the scientific teams gathered at the convention center at the doctor's call was disbelief, then a commotion broke out. Everyone spokes all at once, and probably no one had a chance to hear the other party's arguments.

Instinctively, I grabbed the doctor's hand because the words directed towards me weren't very kind. Some scholars were clearly outraged at my arbitrary actions, but there were those who, to my surprise, stood up for me. Some literally threw themselves at the others – well, maybe not literally, but I was really starting to worry that they would start fighting like little kids. When the discussion started to take dangerous turns, Governor Svennsen appeared on the doorstep of the room, called by who knows who.

"Silence!" her voice rumbled so loudly that everyone fell silent, frightened. "Is this a science conference or a drunken brawl?! What is the meaning of this?!"

Dr. O'Leary, who was obviously enjoying the whole situation, got up from his chair.

"Forgive us, Your Excellency," he began with full, though slightly ridiculing, courtesy. "It's just a dispute over privileges. About who has the right to solve the problem and who does not."

"Nonsense!" one of the biologists shouted. "It's about an irresponsible ignoramus exposing us all to danger!"

"And destroying everything we have achieved so far!" another supported him.

"Be quiet, I didn't give you permission to speak!" Svensson shouted and turned to O'Leary. "Go on, Doctor."

"Miss Solis could not destroy anything, for a simple reason: because so far we have achieved nothing but a fatal misunderstanding," O'Leary said emphatically to the scientists. "Your actions cost us the lives of dozens of people. This girl did nothing wrong, only painted a nice picture and gave it to our opponents. And they reacted and left her a similar gift on the shore. We don't know why they did it, but they did. They are not threatening us any more than before. They still don't come out on dry land. They just know a little more about us and we know a little more about them. That is all."

"Then what's all this shouting for?" the governor asked sarcastically.

"Because none of these great scientists couldn't come up with such an idea of contact. They can't accept the fact that a laboratory assistant has accomplished more than they have."

"That is simply insulting!" Terence Vecksler stood up. "You must be crazy, O'Leary! What are you even accusing us of?!"

"Enough," Svensson said. She walked over to the table and sat down in a seat hastily freed for her by one of the botanists. "Let's stop acting like children. Miss Solis, what did you actually give the Yogs?"

I pulled a copy of my composition from my briefcase and handed it across the table.

"That's very well done," she said, looking at the picture, "and it contains a lot of information. Could I keep it? I would hang it in my office. You had a very reasonable idea, but... why did you not consult with the team?"

I felt embarrassed, my ears stinging.

"I was afraid the scientists would think it's stupid," I muttered, lowering my head.

"You have some complexes," she said rather than asked. "And you don't trust people. Miss Solis, these are serious scholars, not some prima donnas from amateur theater. They don't tear each other's hair out fighting for the lead role. Do you know what the word cooperation means?"

I didn't know what to say, I just looked at her and tears welled up in my eyes. The governor smiled indulgently.

"Don't make yourself out to be a poor little girl. Nobody is putting you in the corner. However, because of you, we have found ourselves in a peculiar situation. You gave something to the Yogs and they repaid the gesture. The problem is that we do not know what this exchange of gifts means in their culture. It could be a gesture of friendship, as you wished, or a declaration of war."

"But how?" I didn't understand. "These are just reproduction patterns."

"Maybe they'll take it as: *There are many of us, and there will be more, and we will crush you,*" she explained patiently. "Or be an obscene insult in their understanding. We don't know. We need to carefully examine the item they left you on the demarcation line and consult on what to do next. For now, you will stay away from the sea. Is that clear?"

"Of course, Your Excellency," I replied dejectedly.

For the rest of the crowd, the governor's words seemed like a cold shower. They visibly calmed down and cooled down.

"I'd say overall, it's a good thing," said biologist Maira Towsend after a while. "Finally, something broke the stalemate we've been stuck at for so long. And we've gained invaluable information about these creatures, haven't we?"

"It needs to be carefully analyzed," Vecksler muttered. His fingers touched the statue in the middle of the table. He was fascinated by it, as were the others.

O'Leary yawned ostentatiously.

"Get to it, then," he said, "and leave my assistant alone. She may have been a little reckless, but she used what you, ladies and gentlemen, lack. Intuition. You ignore her contribution because she doesn't have your diplomas and would fail the simplest test in analytical geometry. Still, I value her more than all of you put together. I'm going back to my work. Get up, Aurita. You don't have to explain anything to these pompous assholes. You're worth too much to be pushed around."

"But I work for them... they hired me..." I protested weakly.

"Wake up, girl!" He tapped my forehead with a bent finger. "You're the one doing them a favor, not the other way around. And if they're unhappy about something, let them illustrate their encyclopedias themselves... as deftly as they have been doing until your arrival."

He took my arm and lifted me almost by force. Overwhelmed by his authority, I followed him and cast only one apologetic look at the scholars gathered in the hall.

O'Leary didn't give me time to think about what I was getting myself into. He quickly got me back to work, of which – honestly speaking – we had a lot of. A team of professionals was needed to build a single android, and here all we've had was the doctor, me, the digital graphic designer Daniel Kazankis, as well as surgeon of artificial shells Leona Hart. Neither of them were very young, rugged, devoted to their passion for creating and friends with O'Leary from the time they worked together on Earth. Together we had to do all the necessary work and in fact each of us had to show different kinds of abilities. Assembling servomotors was a trifle, but what could be called the *android nervous system* required superhuman patience and precision. Artificial muscles were also not easy to obtain and install on the skeleton. Leona Hart was the one who worked on that, carefully selecting and mixing the muscle ingredients.

"Just a small mistake and the muscles won't contract and relax with the right fluidity," she explained when I dared to ask her why she was throwing out seemingly good projects. "Or some will do it with the speed of fifteen milliseconds, while the others sixteen or fourteen and a half milliseconds. That cannot be allowed. That's why they must all be made of one particular portion of mass, not of several or even two different ones."

I understood that perfectly. When I painted, I also tried to use one portion of paint mixed on a palette to paint areas that should have the same shade. When mixing basic colors, it's best not to count on luck to achieve exactly the same color.

"The outer layer, I mean, the skin, is also going to be from one portion?" I asked.

She smiled, amused by my naivety.

"No. After all, the body has different shades, so there is no need for absolute harmony. However, you must know that creating skin for the android is not the same as covering furniture with upholstery. It really is a work of art. And you know what? You'll be of use to me during that, kid."

Those were beautiful days. I felt proud of myself and needed by others. Every day I learned something new, not only in technical matters. I had a better understanding of androids and the fact that they are not like robots made for mass production. Although I could already tell before that Raul was completely different from Roxana 8F belonging to the Denberry family, the extremely handsome Roy 98D, the companion Iman Gossip or even Raina, who walks everywhere like a dog after Astrid. Only now, however, have I understood how great this difference actually is, and why it is there.

While working like this, there was a certain rebelliousness arising in me. I didn't know before that I was capable of such things at all, and yet I was. This was probably a direct result of finding out that I deserved respect as much as any other inhabitant of this colony. Not that I was wiser than a team of experts – but in a situation where scientists with stupidly high IQ and vast knowledge were unable to figure out how to deal with the problem of Yogs, the natives of Patris, maybe it was time to try simpler methods. Ones directly from kindergarten.

Dr. O'Leary had a whole collection of psychological books on memory crystals. He willingly lent them to me and I enjoyed reading. Within them I found the confirmation of something I had learned before, while rummaging in my father's library – communication between cultures, no matter how different, was never impossible for… children. The little ones could always figure out how to find common ground, and soon after they met, they played together, even if they didn't understand each other's words.

"Are you suggesting we send toddlers on a diplomatic mission to the Yogs?" Governor Svensson asked when I secretly went for a visit to her office. I could see the uncertainty in her face as she listened to my reasoning.

"Of course not," I disagreed. "My point is that where science fails, simplicity can prevail. As was the case with my gift. Yes, I know I was irresponsible, but I was able to communicate with them. Like a child giving something to a peer from another world as a sign of friendship, while speaking different languages and growing up in different cultures. I think it's universal. Even some animals offer each other food, for example, and such gestures always mean the same thing."

Svensson nodded.

"There's something to that," she admitted. "What are you getting at?"

Her keen gaze made me feel embarrassed again, but not as much as it used.

"I keep thinking about a certain idea, Your Excellency. It's perfectly safe, but it may seem a little childish. I didn't want to tell the researchers about it, since they would start discussing it, weighing the pros and cons, then they will argue and finally come up with something supposedly based on my original idea, but completely different. And I feel that they will do it all wrong. Because, you see, neither knowledge nor wisdom is needed for this. Just feelings. We won't get them in words or mathematical formulas, and yet I think they'll be of better use when attempting contact with the Yogs. I know, you are about to ask me: how do I know if they have any feelings at all? And I will answer that in a moment. Everything living has them. That's not just my theory, but a scientific fact."

I could tell from the look on her face that she agreed with me.

"Yes, that's true," she said. "I've learned about it. People used to believe that only human beings have feelings and an inner life. It was probably not until the twentieth century that they began to understand that other mammals, birds, reptiles, and even aquatic creatures that still inhabited the seas of the Earth also have them. Unfortunately, this fact was understood too late to save anything... very well then. I don't know what you've come up with and I don't want to know. As long as you promise me to not cross the demarcation line, do what you want, under the condition that I'll get to see the result of the experiment," she smiled." I'm also a scientist. A historian, like your aunt. That's why I support you, albeit quietly for the time being. I am not the only ruler here, but rather the coordinator, and I must be diplomatic. However, in an open confrontation with scholars, you can count on my support.

At first, I didn't know what to think about such kind approach from the most important person in the colony. Then I realized that not everything here was as harmonious as I thought. It occurred to me that Eva Svensson is not necessarily accepted as the governor by everyone. Only now did some parts of conversations, or small pieces of information began to make sense to me... Luis

Goodman, a theoretical physicist, was a candidate with scientific background in the elections and his victory was fiercely fought for. Therefore, Eva must have felt like the oppositionist to the planetologists, biologists and the rest of them. And she certainly wouldn't miss the opportunity to get back at them. That's why she supported me. By no means did this result from pure trust in the not-so-intelligent painter, but from the defiance of the people who voted against Svensson in the election.

Of course, I was silent about this discovery. My mind was now busy with something else: how to complete the plan. It wasn't easy. To do this, I had to get to the coast as inconspicuously as possible, and I had no way of doing so. Normally, I would turn to planetologists, but right now their answer would certainly be no. I didn't want to explain why. I felt a hollow resentment on their part, which they had not yet been able to overcome. Like it or not, I had made a mockery of them, and that's not something they'll forget easily. I couldn't count on their help.

XV

Support came from somewhere else, from a rather unexpected side. I was working on the sketches of the mangrove forest when someone violently knocked on the door.

"It's open!" I shouted.

Jamie burst in. She was wearing tight leggings and a loose top, and a light cape slung over her shoulders. Apparently, the temperature drop didn't affect her. She stumbled against Firefly at the door step, who jumped out to greet her and caused her to stagger.

"Oh geez!" she shouted, regaining her balance. "Do you have your own harpy now? You inherited him from Mr. Ponce, didn't you?"

I put the brush back in a cup of water.

"He needed care after Esteban's death. I liked him anyway, and he likes me. He helped me get through the suicide season. And you spent that time in the dorm, didn't you?"

She sat down on the sofa energetically and threw her slender legs on the back of the chair next to her.

"They force us in there for four weeks every year," she explained casually. "They are sort of like 'half-colonies', so that the adults don't go crazy having to deal with us all day. There's a gloomy atmosphere even in the city, let alone in the estate, where everything is wet twenty-four hours a day. And at the dorm we're dry, warm and happy."

"What do you do there?" I asked, smiling involuntarily.

"Well, during the day we have lessons, scientific experiments and sports activities. And in the evenings, there's dances, board games and so on. No one keeps watch on when we go to sleep, there are no guides and no checks in the bedrooms. And they feed us very well," she looked at a bowl with protein bars standing on my table and grimaced. "Do you live only on this stuff, you poor soul?"

I couldn't help laughing. There was something about this confident, unrestrained kid that it was impossible to stay sad with her. I think she inherited it from her father, because Aunt Estrella, as far as I knew, was more of a closed-off introvert.

"I don't pay much attention to what I eat," I admitted. "I treat it more like a necessity for my body, and that's it. There are other things I have to worry about."

"Yes, I've heard," Jamie became even more lively, if that's even possible. "Apparently you've made the mockery of those busybodies from the planetology team. Everyone in the colony is gossiping about how you solved something in one day that they, a bunch of old, have been struggling with for years to no effect. You don't even know how famous you are. Do you know what Dave says about you? That you've only played pretended to be stupid from the beginning and you're actually smart as a hundred thousand damns. Admit it, aunt, was it really just a game?"

She made me feel embarrassed, and not only because of the very informal language she used.

"Of course not," I said. "I just happened to figure out what needed to be done by chance. I swear. And I didn't really think about it at all. I just suddenly felt like it would be a good idea, and you know..."

"You're amazing," the girl shook her head with admiration. I don't know what impressed her more, my success or rather the audacity with which I ignored all safety regulations at the time. I got an idea.

"Actually, I am planning on doing something else. But I would need some help."

Jamie jumped up from her seat. Her incredibly blue eyes sparkled with excitement. Even a blind man would be able to tell that she was burning with desire for adventure.

"Who do I need to tie up?"

"No one," I assured her quickly. "Can you drive the vehicles here?"

"Oh yes. It's very easy."

"And... will you take me to the sea?"

"Of course!"

"I warn you, though, the planetologists won't like it. Your foster parents may also rub your ears later."

That didn't scare her at all, and I felt it was even the opposite.

"Then that's another reason to help you," she said briskly. "But where are we going to get the vehicle from?"

"From Esteban's property. No one has taken over it yet. It's empty, and the vehicle is behind the house, under the canopy."

"I'll go bring it!"

"No," I took her hand, afraid she would run out before I could fully explain what it was all about. "Not yet. We can't do it right now, it's afternoon and there's too many people. Could you please come pick me up with it before dawn tomorrow? So that we can be at the beach when it's already light outside?"

She must have been a little disappointed. As they say, she was bathed in hot water, didn't like waiting, and liked to act immediately, without delay.

"All right... what are you planning?"

"You'll see. You'll love it. You will have something to tell your friends about."

Overjoyed, she hugged me tightly, patted Firefly on the back and ran outside, singing one of the cheerful songs that often played on the radio. I stared out the window until she was out of sight. Only then did I get back to my sketches. I worked carefully to complete them, thinking about this visit and concluding that I had been wrong before. I had a lot more in common with Jamie than I thought.

The next day I got up when it was still dark and did my morning exercises. Whatever day it was, I always exercised an hour before breakfast and an hour before bed to keep my tendons and my whole body supple. Then I put my long hair in a tight braid and arranged it in a bun in front of the mirror, neatly tying it with long hairpins. When Jamie's vehicle stopped at the door, I was ready. At the sound of the wheels, I grabbed the bag I packed in the evening and jumped out the door. Jamie, sitting behind the wheel, dressed in a black tracksuit and pulled almost over the eyes flat cap, waved at me.

"Get in!" she shouted.

I looked around carefully and grabbed the door handle. At the same moment, a shadow broke away from the house and approached us. It was Raul.

"Did you think I'd let you go alone?" he said as calmly as ever.

"Oh boy," Jamie moaned. "Just what we needed. Do you always have to be stalking people?"

"How did you know?" that's what interested me most at the moment.

"I have good hearing," he replied.

Jamie looked at me questioningly. I shrugged.

"Let him go. What can you do? He's a little overeager, but he could be useful in case of trouble."

"It reminds me of childhood," my cousin stepped on the clutch. "I couldn't go anywhere without that fake buzzkill. You don't even know how embarrassing it was. Everyone would always laugh at me."

"Yes, I can see how that could be annoying," I admitted. "I'm sure none of the girls you were friends with had an android following them around."

"My friends were all boys. Girls are boring, so I preferred to play with boys instead. All they do is talk about clothes and which guy is more attractive. I've never been that interested in fashion."

Strange, it has only now dawned on me that there is something like fashion even in this small colony. The elders probably paid little attention to it, but for adolescent girls it could be an important part of their world. Like on Earth.

"You're always well-dressed anyway," I said.

"Oh, that's thanks to mom Tina. She cares about my wardrobe. She even tried to teach me how-to put-on makeup, but it's such a waste of time... did you notice that mom Tina has pointy ears? They are so pretty. And she always cares about her beauty. She even has an appointment with Dr. Parsons to have her wrinkle surgery done, you know, she's old enough and doesn't want to scare people away," Jamie picked up the gossips as usual and within ten minutes I already knew the embarrassing secrets of everyone around.

Raul was sitting in the back seat and was silent. I was glad he went with us, truth be told, because the road to the sea led through quite wild surroundings and if we became stuck there for one reason or another, the help of the android could prove invaluable. However, I had to admit that despite her young age, Jamie turned out to be a very good driver, although maybe she pressed on the gas too hard. I would have really preferred if she didn't go so fast, but I kept quiet about it.

When we got to the sea, the sun was already over the horizon and it was pouring iridescent rays over everything. The three towers with closed domes stood still, and nothing disturbed them.

"What now?" my companion asked, stopping the car.

"You'll see."

I pulled off my pants and blouse. Underneath I had a leotard brought from Earth. I took the dancer's corset and the lampshade out of my bag. I put them on and tucked the ballet shoes over my feet. I decorated my bun with a tiara. Ignoring Jamie, staring at me open-mouthed, I picked up the music player and ran to the beach.

I placed the player near the demarcation line and turned it on. Stravinsky's music for the *Firebird* ballet burst from the speaker. I tiptoed onto the petrified sand slabs and started my show with *allonge*[6] – I touched my hands together over my head for a moment, facing the towers. Then – when the orchestra momentarily fell silent, and soon after played a lead-in to the solo – I began dancing. I swirled around on the beach, which was actually smooth as a ballroom, with the corner of my eyes seeing Jamie, staring at me, and the towers. I was able to register that all three of the tower's sights had opened and the guards had pushed out what had been their heads through. They were watching me too, and that's what mattered. I didn't know if they could hear the music, but I was sure they could see what I was doing.

Stravinsky's music smoothly transitioned into Grieg's, and I changed the rhythm of the dance. I spent hours preparing this compilation in order to get the greatest variety of melodies and movements. At times, I slightly lost my *aplomb*[7], but I didn't pay attention to it. It wasn't an exam, after all. If there was anything I was worried about, it was that my strength would run out before I finished. Ballet only looks light and airy, but in fact it is hard work that not everyone can cope with and which cripples the dancer in the long run. This is one of the reasons why professional dancers were replaced with holograms as soon as it became possible.

When the last chords from the player finally sounded, I finished the *coda*[8], stopped, facing the towers, and did a *reverence*[9]. Then I straightened up, lowering my right arm vertically down while curving my hand to make the sharpest angle possible with

---

[6] Allongé – a possition in classical ballet (arabesque type), hand position – stretched out unlike *arrondi* (rounded out), the movement is based around extending a closed-off hand position.

[7] Aplomb – ballet coordination.

[8] Coda – the finale of various dance forms, especially as a spectacle.

[9] Révérence – a bow with a squat performed by female dancers.

my forearm. Supposedly a farewell gesture, as claimed by cryptologist Salitzky. Hopefully she was right.

The display of the rather slippery silica plates tired me so much that I barely made it to the car where Jamie was waiting for me.

"That was wonderful! Absolutely amazing!" she grabbed me by the shoulders. "Are you okay, aunt?"

"I'm fine," I exhaled, breathing heavily. "Raul... get the player. Let's go back."

With trembling hands, I took off the outfit and put on my casual clothes.

"I've never seen such a spectacle in my entire life." Jamie turned the ignition key. "You were like a flower, like a butterfly... I bet you have not seen the butterflies here, they appear only in spring. I've seen the Earth ones in a holographic atlas brought by biologists. Could I learn to dance like that?"

I smiled at this naive question.

"It's a little late for that. Learning ballet usually begins when you're a few years old. I was nine and I was still too old to be able to achieve the master level. Although if you want, I can teach you a few basic moves and then we'll see."

"Sounds great!"

Jamie stepped on the gas pedal and began to whistle cheerfully. The prospect of a fight after returning home did not bother her at all, clearly. For my part, I was too exhausted to think about it. My only dream was to find myself in bed and get some rest. My legs hurt so much that I wondered how I could get from the van to my house without stumbling. I took off my ballerinas and struggled to suppress a scream as my toes throbbed in pain and heat.

"You're bleeding," Jamie said worriedly.

"The ballerinas aren't a perfect fit. And I forgot to trim my nails," I explained, trying to keep a relaxed tone. "It's nothing. It will heal quickly. Now imagine what the dancers' feet used to look like after an entire performance."

I hoped that, at least for now, no one would know about our trip, giving me some time to rest. In the meantime, I fell silent. There was something I didn't know – it wasn't just Yogs that had their own watchers. The science department also had them. And they found out about it much faster than I would have liked.

I began to receive videophone calls from the planetologist team before noon. I didn't pick them up, mainly because the videophone was too far from the bed and I couldn't get up. Besides, I didn't want to explain anything to anyone. Raul, who remained to look after me, patiently told each in turn that I was not well. Dr. Polaski came to visit me at home, asked me about my health and gave me an ointment to help the pain in my legs, but I didn't want to see anyone besides her.

I don't know if anyone guessed that I just want to put off the abuse that awaited me. I already received one, as Tina Roberts began speaking on the voice mail, with bitter arguments about dragging my underage cousin into my idiosyncrasy. I suspected that poor Jamie had been grounded for our escapade, since she didn't contact me at all. I avoided talking to anyone all the more, even though I received calls dozen times a day. As a result, the whole team finally invited themselves over for a visit. To my surprise, the planetologists did not seem angry with my doing, but rather worried.

"I don't have anything to offer you," I apologized, trying to get out of bed. My feet still hurt, especially my big toes. However, I didn't have to get up, everyone settled down so easily at my home, as if they were here every day.

"That's all right, we brought cookies. And fruit juice," Sydney Morrows said, showing me a large box full of delicious-looking brownies.

"You have juice? Give it here, I'll make some punch," said Dr. O'Leary, who had arrived with the planetologists. "Raul, come with me to the kitchen, you'll show me where everything is."

He held a bottle of homemade gin, which he brought 'as a gift'. He was known for his moonshine throughout the colony, and whenever someone needed alcohol, they always turned to him.

Less than half an hour had passed, and the whole team was sitting by my bed on folding stools they each had brought (as was the custom, when a larger group gathered somewhere, every person came with their own stool), and in the middle, on the bedside table was my biggest vase, filled with a punch, a box of cookies and a platter with the autumn variety of Patrisian plums. Firefly, exhilarated ran from one person to the next, rubbing against their knees with a coaxing hiss. He was stroked, patted, but it was still not enough. He liked the company of people too much.

Terence Vecksler silenced his colleagues and held up his mug.

"We are gathered here, Miss Solis, to express our appreciation," he began pompously. "I admit, at first we were furious at you. But now..."

I took a sip from my pot. The punch was strong and sweet, I liked it a lot.

"You thought I would only be a convenient tool in your hands," I completed the planetologist's statement. "I don't blame you. Such a stupid girl should have been grateful that you took her under your wing. Looking at it from your point of view, that is logical."

"Don't be so bitter, now," said Shimada, laughing. "Look at it from our point of view. We had reasons to be concerned. But Dr. O'Leary here gave us something to think about..."

"We underestimated the role of intuition in scientific matters," George Benson interrupted him. "We were taught to follow only pure logic in our research. Meanwhile, your childish naivety, forgive me for honesty, turned out to be more valuable in this matter than our diplomas."

I looked at the faces around me.

"Do you want to tell me something?" I said cautiously.

"Sure, they do," O'Leary snorted. He took a sip from his bottle and smiled with satisfaction.

Terence Vecksler gave him a pleading look.

"Allow me, Mac."

"Sure, sure, go ahead. I'll be quiet."

The planetologist cleared his throat and raised the cup again.

"To Aura Maria Solis's health," he said. "From now on a honorary member of our team with full privileges."

I almost dropped the plum I was just about to eat.

"We made First Contact!" I shouted.

"It seems like it. I don't know exactly what kind of message the Yogs read in your beach dance, but the towers are gone. The biologists' motorboat, sent with two volunteers to fetch water samples for the environmental genetics laboratory[10], returned safe, undisturbed by anyone or anything."

"I don't think the content of it is what was important to them," I looked at my guests, overjoyed as never before. "It was probably complete gibberish to them. What mattered was that we tried to make contact by peaceful means. I guess they stopped considering us a threat. Maybe we'll get to know each other better over time."

"Maybe," Sydney agreed. "All of that is ahead of us, Aura Maria. Our entire lives. Cheers!"

---

[10] Environmental genetics – a method of locating living organisms based on their genetic traces in a given environment.

EPILOGUE

I looked at the activated android. He looked exactly like I had imagined my imaginary brother – tall, slender, with light brown skin, high cheekbones, noble features, and black, wire-straight hair with a navy-blue shine. A young Indian, as if taken out of a painting in one of the anthropology textbooks I read in my father's study.

Dr. O'Leary entered the code on the panel of the alcove. The LED lights flickered, and the electrical impulses in the wire network snapped a little, like sparks on a battery's contacts when connecting them together with a wire. The android's eyelids twitched and lifted to reveal pale green irises that illuminated his tawny face. He looked at us quietly, in passive silence.

"Here he is," the doctor said, releasing the alcove's connections to the android body and closing the launcher. He turned to me, "Now it's all up to you. You must teach him the correct use of articulated speech and the rules of social behavior. You have to show him the world. He will depend on you like a child for a while, then he will start to become more independent. Are you ready for this responsibility?"

I nodded almost involuntarily, never taking my eyes off the android's figure, standing still in the alcove. He had exactly the same face as the Indian in my drawing. The doctor's graphic designer programmed the 3D printer to perfection while creating the parts of the outer shell.

"What are you going to call him?" O'Leary asked as the silence began to lengthen. "You can pick any name you want. It doesn't have to begin with an 'R'. We are not on Earth, so we can bend certain rules. So?"

I didn't look at him, but I knew he was smiling. I suppose he understood what I was feeling right now.

I swallowed instinctively before answering.

"Silver. I'll call him... Silver."

THE END